WHERE SECRETS ARE SAFE

JAMEY MOODY

Where Secrets Are Safe

©2021 by Jamey Moody. All rights reserved

Edited: Kat Jackson

This is a work of fiction. Names, characters, places, and incidents are the product of the author's imagination or are used fictitiously. Any resemblance to an actual person, living or dead, business establishments, events, or locales is entirely coincidental.

This book, or part thereof, may not be reproduced in any form without permission.

Thank you for purchasing my book. I hope you enjoy the story.
If you'd like to stay updated on future releases, you can visit my website or sign up for my mailing list here: www.jameymoodyauthor.com.
I'd love to hear from you! Email me at jameymoodyauthor@gmail.com.
As an independent author, reviews are greatly appreciated.

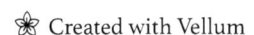

❦ Created with Vellum

CONTENTS

Also by Jamey Moody	v
Chapter 1	1
Chapter 2	8
Chapter 3	15
Chapter 4	22
Chapter 5	30
Chapter 6	36
Chapter 7	42
Chapter 8	49
Chapter 9	59
Chapter 10	65
Chapter 11	73
Chapter 12	80
Chapter 13	88
Chapter 14	97
Chapter 15	106
Chapter 16	115
Chapter 17	123
Chapter 18	129
Chapter 19	136
Chapter 20	143
Chapter 21	149
Chapter 22	155
Chapter 23	160
Chapter 24	169
Chapter 25	177
Chapter 26	185
Chapter 27	193
Chapter 28	200
Chapter 29	209

Three Years Later	213
About the Author	217
Also by Jamey Moody	219
One Little Yes	221

ALSO BY JAMEY MOODY

Live This Love

The Your Way Series:

Finding Home

Finding Family

Finding Forever

It Takes A Miracle

One Little Yes

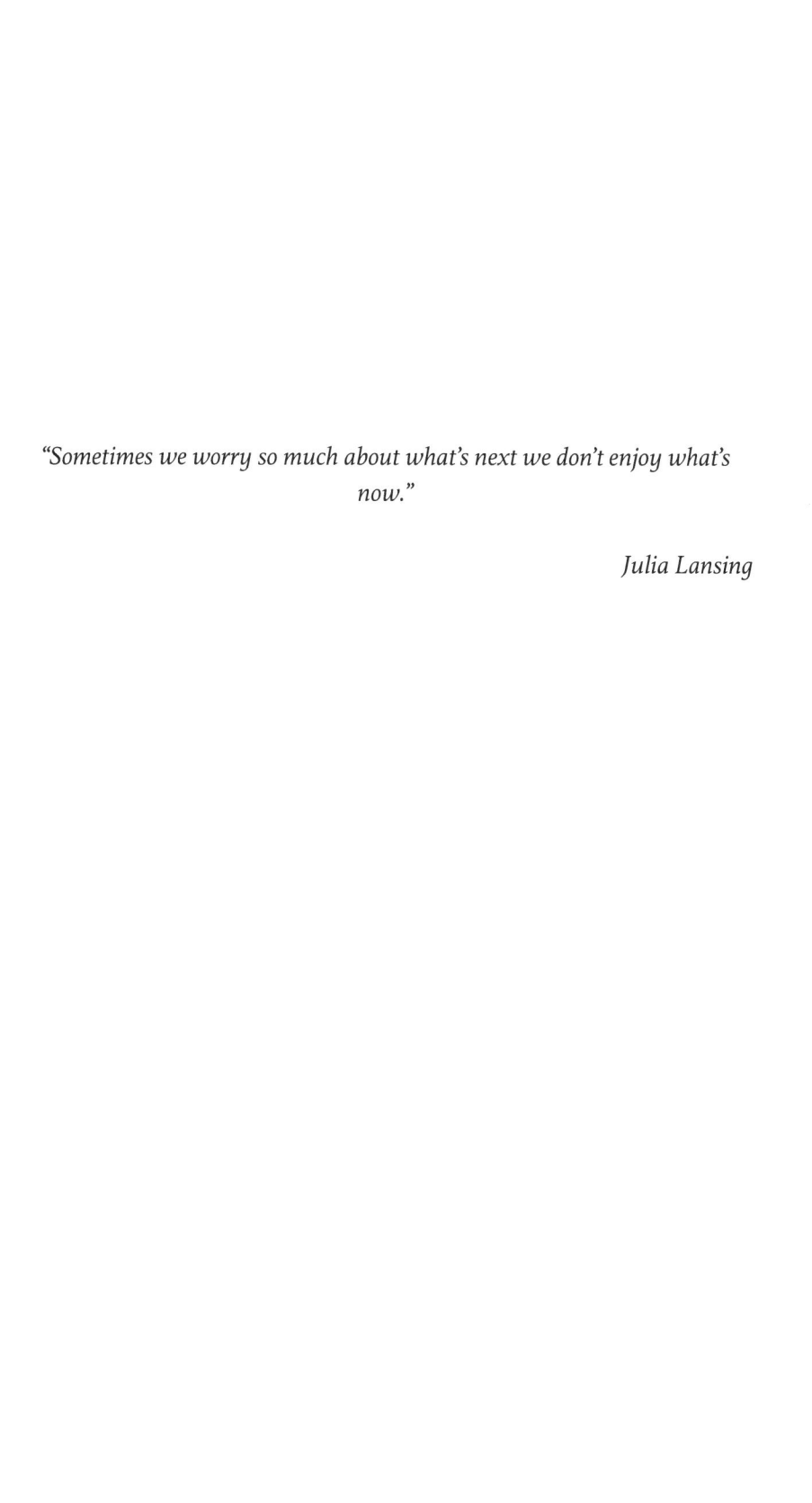

"Sometimes we worry so much about what's next we don't enjoy what's now."

Julia Lansing

1

"Why am I here?" A soft breeze rippled the water with just a hint of coolness, floating over pinkening cheeks.

"I hope you have on sunscreen."

"Sometimes the warmth of the sun on your face is worth the risk," she said, her eyes closed.

"Your adoring fans might not agree."

"That doesn't answer my question. Why have you summoned me home?"

"I didn't summon you home. This is when you usually visit."

"Okay, then why are we sitting at this rundown has-been of a lake resort, drinking beer?"

"We always come here. I can't believe you're speaking so harshly of the setting where many of our happy, coming-of-age memories were made."

"We did have fun, didn't we? We thought we were working a big-time summer job when really all we did was have fun and chase girls." Krista Kyle sighed, fondly remembering those summers over thirty years ago. Her best friend, Julia Lansing, sat next to her now just as she had so many years ago.

"You know it's for sale, right?"

"I did see the sign you pointed at on the way in, yes." Krista nodded with a smirk.

"What would you do with this place? If you could turn it into anything you wanted?" Julia quizzed.

Krista chuckled. "I'd make it a den of lesbian iniquity."

Julia laughed. "I can see it now," she said, sweeping her arm across the landscape. "The Lesbian Lagoon."

"How about the Sapphic Sound," suggested Krista.

"Oh, I know!" Julia exclaimed. "The Hidey Hole." She laughed raucously.

"I've got it. The Babe Bayou," Krista offered, laughing with her.

They sipped their beers, sharing a chuckle.

"If I'd had a place like this all those years ago then maybe I'd have a wife or partner today," Krista said wistfully.

"What? Really?"

"Yeah really. When I first went to Hollywood I had to be careful. I was afraid if the public found out I loved women then my career would be over."

"I'd say it all worked out. You were the favorite friend on the most popular sitcom all through your twenties and most of your thirties. And then in your forties, you became the mother everyone wanted. I think fifty looks good on you *and* me!" Julia stated boldly.

"We do make fifty look good," Krista said, reaching her beer over to clink with Julia's. "You remember Tara?"

"Of course I do. That is one beautiful woman with a spirit to match."

Krista smiled fondly at the compliment of her ex. "We might still be together if there had been someplace we could go to walk along and simply hold hands without someone jumping out, taking a picture, and selling it somewhere. She didn't care what others thought, but her career had already taken off so she didn't have to."

"Do you really think it would have mattered if someone had found out?"

"I do, Jules. It wouldn't be such a big deal now, but thirty years ago it was. Poor Tara hung in there with me for several years, but finally she'd had it."

"I thought she cheated on you!"

"She didn't really cheat. The last straw was when I wouldn't go to a party with her as her date. She was determined to go and went with a date anyway, but it wasn't me. And that, as they say, was that."

"I remember now," Julia said with a faraway look in her eyes. "I wanted to come out there and end her career as the beautiful detective in those spy movies."

Krista chuckled. "That's my Jules. Always defending her friend."

"Best friends since we were born!"

"Anyway, if we could have come here and been ourselves every now and then, maybe Tara would have waited until I was ready to come out."

"At least you were able to do it your way—unlike some people."

"That's true, it simply wasn't fast enough for Tara." Krista turned to Julia suddenly. "Did I tell you that right before I did my coming out interview the 'out reporter' contacted me?" she said, making air quotes with her fingers.

"Brooke what's-her-name?"

"Yeah, Brooke Bell. She said she'd heard some rumors about me and several close friends of mine corroborated them."

"No way!"

"Yeah, that's what journalists like her do. They try to get you to out yourself. I called bullshit and told her she was late to the party, but not before I let her know what a terrible person she was for treating people that way."

"Good for you!"

"I do love this place," Krista said, sitting up and looking around. "How many cabins are here?"

"I think there are ten."

"Hmm, I wonder if those hiking trails are still maintained and what shape the beach is in," she said as much to herself as to Julia. She stood up and looked out to where the water met the sand. "It doesn't look too bad from here."

A smile crept onto Julia's face. "Are you going to buy it?"

Krista looked down at her, responding to her smile with a mischievous one of her own. "Maybe."

"Are there really that many closeted people out there looking for a place like this?"

"Well, not the way this place is right now, but maybe after I fix it up. To answer your question, yes—there are people that are very private about their sexuality and want to keep it that way. And not just in Hollywood."

"What do you mean?"

"You'd be surprised at the number of people that don't want their sexuality to come out because of their profession or their family."

"So this place could be where they come to live their secrets. Where their secrets are safe?"

"Exactly!"

"Hmm, and how do you propose to keep others from finding out what you're doing here?"

"Easy," Krista said. "The lake community watches out for one another. They don't care if a bunch of lesbians come here to have a good time as long as they're respectful, take care of the lake, and keep to themselves. You know that."

"That's true. There was that famous pop star that rented the Richardson's place to write songs and no one ever knew she was here. She shopped in town, hiked the trails, and no one said a word. I think she was here for six months!"

"What about when we were in college and came back to work that summer and George Clooney rented a house for a month? He had different people here every week. And no one said a word."

"Nope. Wait a minute," Julia said, turning to Krista. "You're really going to do this," she said as her face lit up.

"Isn't that why you asked me to come home?" Krista deadpanned.

"Well yeah, but I didn't think you'd do it," she said, laughing.

"Yes you did. When have I ever not done what you suggested?" Krista said, shaking her head.

"Well," Julia said, looking up. "There was that time…" she said trailing off.

"I know what you're going to say. I should have gone after Melanie and I didn't, but that was years ago. I'm sorry I didn't listen and I missed my chance to be with my first love. Since then I've listened to you."

"Young love; that was such a hard lesson."

They stared at one another, both thinking of the past. Krista smiled and clapped her hands. "Okay. Let's buy this rundown resort and make it our very own Hideaway Cove. Who has it listed?"

"Your old friend, Lauren Nichols. I bet if you offer to spend the weekend with her she'd get you a better deal," said Julia.

"What? Lauren Nichols?"

"You know she's always had a thing for you, especially after you came out."

"I did not know that. We were friends in high school. Besides, she's married."

"That doesn't matter."

"It does to me!"

"Okay, okay," Julia said, raising her hands and holding them up toward Krista. "Just keep in mind she likes you."

Krista looked at her but didn't say anything.

"Hey, does this mean you're moving back here?" Julia said, clapping her hands.

"No, I'm not moving back. I mean, I'll be here more often, but I still have projects in LA."

"Then who's going to run it?"

A sly smile split Krista's face. "You are."

"Me!" Julia said, pointing to herself.

"Yes you. Who else is going to do it? Besides, you're not doing anything."

"I'm not doing anything because I've been an exceptional mother and raised my two girls to be independent and now finally, they're both in college. It's my time now!"

"And what does Heidi have to say about that?

"My wife knows how valuable my time is and how hard I've worked."

Krista gave her a skeptical look. "Oh does she?"

"She certainly does."

"Hmm," Krista said, getting her phone out. "Let me just give her a call." She wrinkled her nose.

Before the call connected a car pulled up next to the deck. Heidi got out of the car and waved.

"Look who's here. I can ask her in person," Krista said, standing up to greet her friend.

"Ask me what?' she said, pulling Krista into a hug. "I'm so glad to see you."

Krista smiled at Heidi. "You are even more beautiful than the last time I was here."

"You say that everytime you come home," Heidi said, leaning over and giving Julia a kiss.

"Because it's true!"

"It's because she has a wonderful wife that treats her like the queen she is," Julia said, winking at Heidi.

Heidi smiled down at her then looked at Krista. "Has she talked you into buying this place?"

"Only if she'll run it," Krista said, handing Heidi a beer.

"I can't think of anyone better," Heidi agreed.

"What!" Julia said, sitting up. "The girls have barely gone back to school. I have plans."

"Plans?" Krista looked at her in disbelief.

"Darling, I don't remember you sharing any plans," Heidi said.

"I most certainly did. I told you I wasn't doing a damn thing!"

"Oh." Heidi chuckled. "I do remember that."

"Be serious, Jules. When have you ever simply sat around? You're always doing something. And this," Krista said, spreading her arms wide, "this is our something."

Julia looked at her suspiciously. "Our something?"

"Yes. There's no way I'd attempt this if you weren't in it with me."

A grin grew on Julia's face. She looked at Heidi and then at Krista. "This really could be a lot of fun."

"Yeah it could." Krista grinned back at her.

"Then you'd better call your girlfriend and get her out here."

"Girlfriend?" Heidi asked.

"Lauren Nichols. You know she has the hots for Krissy."

Heidi nodded. "She does!"

"Not you, too! No she doesn't!" exclaimed Krista as she found the real estate listing in her phone and made the call. She asked for Lauren and waited, her foot tapping impatiently.

"Hi Lauren. This is Krista Kyle. I wanted to–" she began.

"Krista! How are you? It's been ages!" Lauren Nichols exclaimed. "How can I help you?"

Krista blinked a few times at Lauren's enthusiasm. "It has been ages," she agreed. "Actually, I'm out at the old Bailey place on the lake and wondered if you could show me around?"

"What! I'd love to! Let me see." Krista could hear papers rustling. "I can be there in thirty minutes. Would that work?"

"I'll be waiting." Krista grinned.

Julia and Heidi shook their heads in unison at her.

"See you soon," Lauren said, breathless.

Krista slipped her phone into her pocket and looked at her friends. "She'll be here in thirty minutes."

2

"She sounded rather excited on the phone." Julia smirked.

Krista pursed her lips. "I'm sure she's excited to have a nibble on this place. I can't imagine she's had many offers."

"Right. I'm sure that's it," Julia said, taking a sip of her beer.

Krista reached for another beer and walked toward the beach. Memories flooded her mind. She could hear laughter and water splashing just like it was yesterday.

Julia walked up beside her. "Do you remember when those Italian women came and stayed for a week?"

"Of course I do. That was the first time we'd ever seen two women actually hold hands. We'd seen it on TV or in magazines, but not right in front of our eyes," Krista recalled.

"I didn't want to stare, but I couldn't keep my eyes off them."

"I know! Me too!" Krista exclaimed. "I think that was the first time that I realized I could do that. That someday that could be me."

"Yeah. Before that it was like a dream."

"I couldn't wait to go to college. I just knew there had to be other girls like me there."

"I remember they were swimming and then ran back to their

towels on the beach. They sat down and one leaned over and kissed the other. My heart nearly beat out of my chest! I felt like I was the one that had been kissed."

Krista laughed. "And then they saw us staring. My face was so red!"

"What did they do then?" Heidi asked, listening to the memory.

"They winked at us!" Julia chuckled.

"Yep and then we ran," Krista said.

"Ran?" asked Heidi.

"We didn't really run, but we hurried to the dock and busied ourselves with the boats," Krista explained.

"They were really nice and didn't seem bothered by our attention," said Julia.

Krista came back to the present and turned to Heidi. "I could use your legal skills to look all of this over."

"I'd be happy to, but what exactly do you plan to do with this place?"

"She's going to turn it into a lesbian brothel," Julia said with a straight face.

"Right," Heidi said, unconvinced.

"We're calling it the Hidey Hole," Krista said, just as serious.

Heidi looked from Julia to Krista and back. "I see that smile at the corner of your mouth." Julia and Krista laughed loudly. "You nearly had me," Heidi added, laughing with them.

Krista explained to Heidi what her vision for the place was.

After a few moments Heidi asked, "That all sounds great, but how are you going to screen who comes in? I mean, are you advertising it as gay-friendly or what?"

"I'm not advertising at all. It will be strictly word of mouth. Believe me, I know most of the closeted queers in LA. I'll look over the reservation list and if there's someone I don't know, my assistant can find out all about them."

"Your assistant?"

"Yeah, you remember Presley. She's incredible. That woman can find out anything about anyone, like the time you had a fight on the playground back in fifth grade. I don't know how she does it, but she's the master of background checks."

"Hmm," Heidi murmured in thought.

"What?" Krista asked.

"I'm just trying to picture how this is going to work."

"I'll tell a few friends that I've got this great exclusive, private place in Texas. Contact me if you're interested."

"Okay. Let's say five couples are scheduled for the first week in April. What do they do?"

"They fly to the Dallas Fort Worth Airport where we will pick them up. We drive them here, set them up in their cabins, and tell them about the activities available. They do whatever they want, respectfully. I mean, I can't have them fucking on the beach in broad daylight. That would be a bit much."

"Maybe not broad daylight, but I'm sure it's happened before and will again," Julia said. "That beach is kind of perfect in the moonlight."

A slow smile crept onto Krista's face. "Is there something you need to tell us?"

"No there is not," Julia scoffed. "But I will say this. Be ready, my love," she said, turning to Heidi and putting her hands on her hips. "We can sneak down to the beach one night. I know the owner." She pecked Heidi on the lips.

They were all laughing when they heard gravel crunching. Turning toward the deck they saw a car pull up next to Heidi's. Lauren Nichols got out and waved.

They walked up to meet her and she immediately smiled at Krista. "Krista Kyle, how do you get more beautiful?"

Krista smiled a bit timidly. Compliments like this unnerved her sometimes. She'd never considered herself beautiful. She had full, rich, mahogany brown hair that she took care of. Early on she knew it was a hereditary favor and she appreciated it. Her crystal clear blue eyes were also a gift of good genes she had thanked her grandmother for many times.

"Thank you, Lauren, but I could ask you the same question."

Lauren scoffed and looked down. "Now you're just being nice." She looked back up at Krista. "You were always so nice."

Krista smiled at her.

"It's nice to see you, Lauren," Julia said, speaking up.

Lauren looked over and smiled. "It's always nice to see you, Julia." Then she made eye contact with Heidi. "And you too, Heidi."

With the greetings out of the way Lauren turned back to Krista. "Since it's such a nice day for March, let's go look at the cabins by the lake first."

Krista walked next to Lauren as Julia and Heidi followed behind them.

"Do you have a realtor?" Lauren asked as they walked to the first cabin.

"No. Your sign was at the gate when we came in so I called you."

"What I mean is, if you're looking for a certain kind of property, I'd be happy to help."

"I'll keep that in mind, but I hope this one doesn't need too much updating."

"Are you looking to move back home?" Lauren asked, unable to keep the excitement from her voice.

"Not exactly. But I hope to spend more time here."

Lauren unlocked the door and walked in, holding the door for the others.

"This is one of the larger cabins and was updated a few years ago," Lauren said, walking into the middle of the room.

"Wow. This looks better than I thought it would," Julia said, walking to the door of the separate bedroom.

"Did you plan to open it as a resort, Krista?" Lauren asked.

Krista walked to the kitchenette and looked out the window. She could just see the deck and restaurant through the trees. "I'm not sure. It would be a fun place to bring a group of friends."

"Or big families could buy out the place for the week or weekend," suggested Julia.

"Are you looking for an investment? Because I have other properties that would be perfect for that," Lauren said.

Krista smiled at her. "Thanks, Lauren. You're not trying to steer me away from here, are you?"

"Not at all," Lauren answered quickly. "I simply want you to get the property that fits your needs."

"That's nice of you."

"She's doing her job," Julia pointed out.

"I am, but I'm also your friend and want what's best for you," Lauren declared.

"Thanks Lauren, I appreciate that."

"Come on, we have a lot to see," she said.

They walked out and looked at the rest of the cabins. Some were in better shape than others. Krista took a few notes and followed the group out on the dock.

"The Baileys reworked the dock two years ago," Lauren said.

There were several slips to tie boats in on one end. On the other end was a double deck for sunbathing on top and a diving board on the bottom. Between the dock and the shore was an area roped off for swimming.

"We sure would've had fun on this," Julia said, walking up the stairs to the top deck.

"We had fun on the old dock," said Krista.

"Oh that's right. I forgot that y'all worked here in the summers," said Lauren.

"We thought it was work at the time, but now all I remember is fun." Krista grinned.

"I don't remember hauling trash being fun," said Julia.

"Picking up trash on the beach sure was. I seem to recall you trying to pick up more than cans and bottles," Krista teased.

"Tell me more," Heidi said, chuckling.

"I did not! I wasn't brave enough then."

Krista laughed at her friend. "You sure wanted to though, didn't you?"

Julia laughed with her. "You did too."

"You both knew then?" asked Lauren.

Krista and Julia turned to her.

"I'm sorry! Was that offensive?" Lauren blushed.

"Not at all," Krista assured her. "Yes, I knew when I was in high school, but didn't think anyone else was like me."

"You knew I was!" exclaimed Julia.

Krista turned to her. "You were my best friend. I didn't want to kiss you!"

"Who did you want to kiss?" teased Heidi.

Krista looked out over the water back toward the beach. "You know, that pavilion area would be the perfect place for a firepit," she said, changing the subject.

"Okay then. I'll just have to get Julia to tell me your secrets later," said Heidi.

"Good luck with that," Krista said, winking. She noticed Lauren was engrossed in their conversation and hanging on each word. "Can we look at the restaurant now?"

"Sure," Lauren said, snapping back to attention.

As they walked up to the building Krista said, "I hope we didn't make you uncomfortable back there."

"Not at all. It's interesting to me. I can imagine it was difficult for you." She glanced over at Krista.

"It was hard for all of us at that age, wasn't it?"

"I guess you're right. Most of us were just trying to fit in."

"Or trying to find our people."

Lauren didn't say anything more and unlocked the door to the main building that also housed the restaurant.

She showed them the restaurant, kitchen, and bar area. They walked around taking it all in.

Finally Krista said, "Lauren, would you mind meeting me out here again this week? I'd like my cousin to come out and look around."

"Do you mean Brian? He does such good work. I recommend him whenever a client is looking for a contractor."

"I'd like him to give me his opinion if you wouldn't mind."

"I'd be happy to meet you out here. Let me know when and I'll be here," she said enthusiastically.

Krista wasn't sure if she did this for all her clients or if Julia and Heidi were right. Maybe Lauren Nichols had a little crush on her.

3

The next day Krista drove through the entrance to Bailey's Camp on the Lake, as it was still known. She never was sure why they called it a camp unless many years ago when it first opened there were only campsites and no cabins. She parked down by the beach where two weathered adirondack chairs sat. She hoped they were still sturdy.

She got out and looked out over the sparkling water. A deep inhale followed by a slow exhale gently eased any tension in her body. There was something about this place that always calmed her. The idea of owning it had blossomed into a real possibility overnight. Turning this beautiful haven into a safe harbor for those that were afraid to be themselves in public for whatever reason had given her a new direction.

Krista's looks, talent, and a few lucky breaks had given her a profitable career. She was in a position now to pick and choose projects she wanted to be in. Realistically, she could never work again and still have more money than she could ever spend. But she wasn't ready to fade away just yet. There were more roles now for gay men and women and they didn't automatically die or end with broken hearts as they had in the past.

She remembered how it felt to go to events and be expected to bring a man as a date. Later there would be an after party where she and Tara would meet. In the beginning it didn't bother her because she figured it was the price they had to pay. But when she and Tara ended their relationship, the hiding and secret keeping weighed her down to the point that she stopped taking dates to any of the award ceremonies or public appearances.

There had been a couple of relationships that lasted more than two years, but not much longer than that. She thought coming out would make these events bearable, and it had helped, but she simply hadn't found the woman to spend her life with yet. The notion that she could provide a place where those hiding could come and love one another openly made her heart happy.

The hum of a car grabbed her attention away from the water and her thoughts. She turned to see a pickup truck followed by a car making their way down to where she sat.

"Hey Krissy," her cousin Brian said, coming over to give her a hug.

"Hi Bri. Thanks for doing this."

"No problem."

Lauren joined them. "Hi Krista. Hi Brian."

"Lauren," Brian nodded.

"Thanks again for showing us around today, Lauren," Krista said.

"I'm happy to."

"Actually, would it be all right if I looked around on my own?" Brian asked.

Krista looked at him, her brow furrowed.

"It would be best for me to get an idea of what you've got here. Then we can sit down and you can ask questions and I can give you my assessment."

"That's fine with me," Krista said, relaxing. "I don't need to follow you around."

"I don't have to either. I'll give you the keys," Lauren offered.

She showed Brian the keys to the different buildings and he walked away.

"Care to join me?" Krista asked, pointing to the chairs. "They're sturdier than they look," she assured Lauren.

"Sure," Lauren said, sitting back in one of the chairs. "It's another beautiful day. You have calmed the March winds."

"I don't know about that." Krista chuckled.

"Do you have something in mind you want to do with this place? Because I can't see you coming back here to run a lake resort."

"You don't?" teased Krista. "That's why I'm going to recruit Julia to run it."

"Hmm, are you going to make it a place for the gay community?"

Krista eyed Lauren curiously. "Do you think that would be a problem?"

"No. You know how the lake folks are. As long as you take care of your business they aren't going to bother you."

"What about the town folks?"

"You're well respected in town, Krista. I don't see that being a problem either."

Krista nodded, appreciating Lauren's opinion since she lived and worked there. "Would you mind not saying anything just yet? I'm not exactly sure what I may run into legally. Heidi is going to look into that for me."

"Heidi is the best. I won't say a word. Besides, it's no one's business but yours."

"Thanks Lauren. I appreciate it. Hey, I meant to ask you yesterday. How's Marcus?"

"Marcus is fine," she said with a bit of disdain.

"Okay...?"

Lauren looked over at her. "I shouldn't have said it like that. He's fine, the kids are fine."

"I was about to ask about Emily and Justin."

"Emily will graduate this year and Justin's been living in Dallas for three years, working his way up the corporate ladder."

"You must be proud."

"I am. The kids are independent and know what they want."

"Why do you sound unhappy? I know you want them to excel."

"I do. It's just that since they are on their own, some things about my relationship with Marcus have been uncovered. Let me ask you," she said, looking at Krista. "Maybe I'm expecting too much, but the only things Marcus is passionate about are fishing and watching the Cowboys during football season. We have nothing in common except the kids."

"Oh. Well I'm not the best person to ask since I'm sitting here at fifty with a few relationships that lasted two years, but no more. However, I haven't given up hope of finding the woman to spend the rest of my life with. And I also plan to be passionate with and about this person until the day I die."

"Maybe I've watched too many Hallmark movies and read too many romance novels, but I believe there has to be more. Just because we're older doesn't mean we don't want to—you know," Lauren said.

Krista smiled. "Whatever do you mean?" she teased.

"You know what I mean," Lauren scoffed.

Krista chuckled. "Yeah, you mean have wild, passionate sex! I totally agree with you."

"But it's scary. I mean, do I throw away what I've known for over thirty years?"

"As I said, I'm not the one to ask. You should talk to Julia and Heidi. They are still crazy for one another. I hoped to have that someday. It's obviously taken me a little longer to find it. Have you thought about counseling?"

"I have. It's not like we aren't friends. There's simply not a spark there anymore. It's made me look at myself differently."

Krista gazed at Lauren kindly. "You have a lot of living left to do. We both do."

Lauren nodded and smiled back at her. They both heard Brian walk up before they saw him.

"Well, it isn't as bad as I thought," he said, sitting on the sand in front of them.

"Is that a good thing?" asked Krista.

He chuckled. "Yeah, it is. When were you hoping to open?"

"I'd like to by the middle of May."

Brian looked over at the cabins and then up to the restaurant. Krista could see the calculations running through his head.

"I think that's doable. We can sit down and prioritize, but I'm sure you'll be able to open in May. You may not be at full capacity, though."

"I don't plan to have all the cabins rented at the same time. I think that would be too many people for what I want to do."

"Okay. Let me work up a plan and come see me tomorrow," he said, getting to his feet.

"Thanks Brian. I really appreciate it," Krista said, getting up and hugging him.

"Here you go," he said, handing Lauren the keys. "See you tomorrow."

Krista turned to Lauren. "Well, I want to talk to Heidi. Then I'll call you with an offer."

Lauren clapped. "That's wonderful! The best part is that you'll be home more."

"Thanks Lauren. That's kind of you, but we haven't settled on a price yet."

"We will. I'm sure of it."

They walked to their cars and before Krista got in she looked over the roof of her car at Lauren. "You deserve more, Lauren. I hope you find it."

Lauren smiled. "Thanks Krista. I hope to hear from you tomorrow?"

"You will. Bye," she said, a hint of her Texas accent slipping through.

* * *

"Lauren thought it was a good offer and felt sure the Baileys would agree," Krista said. She and Julia had met Heidi at her office and were waiting to hear back from Lauren.

"I thought it was fair to the Baileys and it's within your budget to renovate and open by May," agreed Heidi.

Julia eyed Krista. "You are staying to help with the renovation decisions, right?"

Krista chuckled. "What's the matter? You know you're the one with the design eye. You don't need me."

"Hell I don't! It's your secret hideaway."

"I'll be here the rest of the month. I have to go back in April for a guest spot and also to start promoting."

"I'm still not sure how you're going to do that, but that's your expertise. What am I supposed to say if someone around here asks for reservations?"

"Give them the Hidey Hole email address," Krista said, giggling.

Heidi shook her head. "Y'all have got to stop calling it that."

"Have we settled on a name?" asked Julia.

"I kind of like Lovers Landing. I hope that's what will be happening. Lovers come here to be together unapologetically and openly," said Krista.

"Do you think that would attract honeymooners?" Heidi asked.

"Any name we choose will have pros and cons," stated Julia. "Do you need to name it something neutral to protect those with secrets?"

"They'll know their secrets are safe or they wouldn't come here in the first place," Krista pointed out.

"Then I like Lovers Landing," said Julia.

"Me too," Heidi agreed.

Krista's ringtone interrupted the discussion. She looked at her screen and raised her eyebrows. "It's Lauren. Fingers crossed Lovers Landing is ours."

She connected the call. "Hi Lauren, I've got you on speaker."

"Have you ever owned your very own lake resort?" Lauren asked cheerily.

Krista smiled. "I'm trying to."

"Well, I heard this gorgeous Hollywood star is buying Bailey's Camp," she teased.

"Is that right?"

"It is if I can get her to agree to one concession," Lauren said.

"And what would that be?" Krista asked, her heart thumping in her chest.

"Your real estate agent gets a tour after you finish the renovations."

The smile on Krista's face lit the room. "My real estate agent is welcome anytime."

"Then let me be the first to congratulate you! Krista Kyle, you are the new owner of a lake resort," Lauren said, her voice rising in enthusiasm.

Julia and Heidi began to cheer and applaud as Krista released the breath she'd been holding.

"Thank you, Lauren!"

"It's my pleasure. I didn't have to do much, though; you gave them a fair offer. I'll get the inspection and title work started."

"Thank you so much, Lauren."

"You're very welcome. I'll be in touch."

Krista turned to Julia and said, "Here we go!"

They embraced and laughed a bit nervously.

"I remember nearly every day one of us would say, 'If I owned this place, I'd do this' and now you do!" Julia said, hugging Krista again.

"Actually, so do you," Krista said.

"What?"

"Jules, I couldn't do this without you. We're in this together. I'll put up the money, but you're the one that's going to be here running the day to day most of the time."

Julia stared at Krista for several moments. "Are you sure?"

"Of course I'm sure," Krista answered quickly. "Partner?" she said, holding out her hand to Julia.

"Partner." Julia grinned, shaking Krista's hand.

Now the real work began.

4

On May 10th, Lovers Landing officially opened. Krista and Julia picked up four couples from the airport and whisked them away to the lake. Eight of the ten cabins were fully functional, and Krista had had one cabin renovated just for her. This was her haven while she was there working. She'd hired two full time maintenance employees with one living on site who was available for anything that came up at night. The restaurant chef and staff were ready and couldn't wait to delight the women with their creations.

A multicolored cat that wasn't a typical calico wandered up as the guests got out of the van. She welcomed them with a meow and then sat watching as if appraising each person.

"Who is this?" the last guest asked as she exited the van.

"This is Sappho. She wandered up and made us her home. Feel free to spoil her; she'll reward you with the best purrs," Krista said, smiling at the cat.

Four golf carts were lined up and ready for the guests. Julia directed each couple to their assigned cart with a driver that would take them to their cabins. A map of the resort was provided along with a description of the grounds and a list of all the activities offered.

Once delivered to their lake homes for the week, the twosomes were given a rundown of what the resort provided. Above all their hosts emphasized how important it was to Lovers Landing that they have a good time without any worries.

Krista and Julia met back at the restaurant and looked at one another anxiously.

"What do you think?" Julia asked nervously.

"Everyone seemed excited, but relaxed. I think it's going to be okay," Krista answered.

"Okay? It needs to be better than okay!"

Krista laughed. "It will be." She looked around and then back at Julia. "I can't believe we really did it."

Julia grinned. "I'm proud of us."

"I am too," Krista said, hugging her.

"I'm going inside to make sure everything is ready in the kitchen," Julia said, letting Krista go.

"I'm going to the beach to double check the bar is stocked and then to the dock."

"I'll meet you there."

Krista nodded and smiled. "Take a breath, Jules. We can do this."

Julia did as she was told. "We are doing this," she said, exhaling.

They were both right. The week passed without any major problems. The couples had a peaceful, restorative week and all promised to return. Their return to their LA social groups was the best kind of advertising. The guests assured Krista and Julia they would be discreet as they wanted this little oasis to thrive.

The summer passed quickly without incident. Everyone got better at their jobs, including Krista and Julia. They'd had no idea how much they would enjoy their new roles. When they watched each new group begin to relax and walk around the property hand in hand accompanied by laughter, it made their hearts swell.

"Look at them," Julia said, nodding toward a couple walking out into the water holding hands. When they were chest deep they put their arms around one another and shared a kiss.

"It's beautiful," sighed Krista.

"It is. I can't believe how happy it makes me to see that."

"I know. This place has become exactly what we hoped."

Julia glanced over at Krista and smiled. They were sitting on the deck in the same place they were back in March when Lovers Landing was created.

"I'll miss you next week," Julia said.

"No you won't. You'll have a chance to stay home and get away from this place and rest."

Julia laughed.

"The best thing we did was give ourselves several days between groups," said Krista.

Julia nodded. "I'll still miss you. You're coming back with the next group, right?"

"That's the plan. That reminds me, I've got to see who is in the next group. Presley took a couple of days off. I'll get the list when I get to LA tomorrow night."

"Have fun at the party. I can't wait to see the pictures the next day."

Krista chuckled. "I'm not sure this will get that kind of coverage. It's an LGBTQ+ fundraising event and they throw a good party, but you never know." Krista got up and looked down at Julia. "I'm going to pack. Why don't you go home early? I can handle everything tonight."

"Okay. I'll see you in the morning."

Krista winked at her friend and walked toward her cabin.

* * *

Krista sat on her back porch and looked out over her backyard and down into the canyon that bordered her property. It was a killer view when the weather cooperated and especially beautiful at night when the lights of LA twinkled below.

She didn't necessarily miss LA, but she did miss this vista and a few people she considered friends. Lovers Landing had enabled her to stay in Texas and return to LA when she had to work. This gave her a renewed energy toward the business that had been mostly good to her. Knowing that she would be here a short time made the projects she was involved in exciting and bearable.

Her phone pinged announcing Presley's, her trusted assistant, arrival. She would let herself in and make her way to the backyard, knowing it was where Krista spent the majority of her time when she was home.

"Good morning," Presley said cheerily, walking through the open French doors.

Krista stood up smiling and held her arms open to her assistant and friend. Presley was twenty-nine, but had been working for Krista since she'd arrived in LA at the tender age of twenty-one. Eight years was a long time in an industry like Hollywood. She was grateful to have Presley's expertise and loyalty. But over the years they had developed a friendship that was comforting to them both.

Presley walked into Krista's arms and they held one another for a moment. Krista took a step back and looked at her friend from top to bottom. "What's different about you?" she said, tilting her head and putting a finger to her mouth.

Presley smirked and waited.

"Hmm, I've got it, I like the hair. And is that a new tattoo?"

Presley smiled appreciatively. "It is. Thank you for noticing," she said, holding out her arm to give Krista a closer look.

"I love the colors," Krista said, turning Presley's forearm over and looking at the rainbow flag that now adorned her arm just above the wrist. "Are you letting your hair grow out?" she asked, letting go of her arm.

"Yeah. I wanted to see if I could swoop it over."

"It's good now, but when it gets a little longer, watch out," Krista said, perusing the new hairstyle.

"Thanks," Presley said, sitting in the chair next to Krista's.

"Okay, give me the details about the week," Krista said, pouring water over ice and adding lemon slices. She set the glass next to Presley's laptop as she tapped away on the keys.

"A fresh new stylist wants to dress you for the fundraiser," Presley said, still tapping on the keyboard.

"Me? Why me?"

Presley stole a quick look at Krista and pursed her lips. "Why does anyone do something like that? She's trying to get noticed. But I happen to know that she likes you and has been a fan for years."

"If she's been a fan for years then why hasn't she already been noticed?"

Presley stopped tapping and looked up at Krista. "She said something about you being a project for a course she took in design school."

Krista furrowed her brow. "What aren't you telling me, Presley?"

She uncrossed and recrossed her legs. "Well, here's the thing. She has been a fan for years and you were her project in school, but she didn't have any way to get in to see you."

"Uh huh, until?"

"Until..." Presley said, obviously uncomfortable.

Realization dawned on Krista's face. "Until she got to know my extremely hot and charming assistant." Krista smirked. "Am I close?"

Presley nodded. "You are, but I would never even mention her if I didn't think she was good. I'm telling you, Krista, she's amazing."

Krista chuckled. "Oh, I'm sure she is, but does she have any design talent?"

"Very funny," Presley said, her cheeks reddening. "I thought it might be fun for you. It's been ages since you let anyone dress you for an event."

Krista scoffed. "Because I don't go to events like that anymore."

"You are this week," Presley pointed out.

Krista studied her assistant. Presley usually ran interference for Krista and was selective on who was actually granted an appointment. She trusted Presley and knew she wouldn't suggest it if this designer didn't have some talent. "Okay. Set it up."

Presley's head shot up and she met Krista's eyes. "I will," she said, quickly tapping on the keyboard once again before Krista changed her mind. A small smile played across Presley's lips and Krista grinned. She had a feeling this designer may have been the reason Presley had taken a few days off.

"Okay. She'll be here tomorrow afternoon," Presley said, looking up at Krista.

"Good. You'll be here too, won't you?" Krista said, trying to keep a straight face.

"Of course. If you need me," Presley said with a look that was all business.

"I'll need you," Krista said, not able to contain her smile.

Presley couldn't help smiling back at her.

"What's next? Do you have the list for the next group going to Texas?"

"I do," Presley said, looking back down at her laptop. "We have four couples. Two have been there before, one is new, but you know them." Presley turned the screen toward Krista so she could see the list.

Krista smiled. "I do know them. I'm happy and surprised they'll be joining us. Talk about being careful. These two have been in the closet so long it's more like a hidden bunker complete with security codes." She stared at the other two names on the list.

"I don't know about these two. There's something odd," Presley said.

"Go on," encouraged Krista.

"At first it was just one of them that contacted us for reservations. I explained that it was only for couples."

"What happened then?"

"She made up some kind of story that she thought one name meant reservations for two people."

"I guess that could happen."

"When I asked for photos she wanted to know why. I explained our security procedures and said the reservation couldn't be made without photos. I had the feeling that she either found a friend to come with her or an escort."

"What made you think that?"

"I don't know, Krista. Something just doesn't feel right."

"Have you done background checks yet?"

"No. I just got the photos this morning. One of them looks familiar, but the photos are vague. Take a look," Presley said, once again turning the screen to Krista.

"Hmm," Krista murmured. Something about the blonde made the hairs on the back of Krista's neck stand up. Then it hit her. "Oh my God," she said quietly. "That's Brooke Bell. Fuck me," she sighed.

"Brooke Bell? You think?" Presley said, peering at the picture.

"Yep. That's her. She probably knows just enough about Lovers Landing to hide her face from me." Krista exhaled an exasperated breath. "Damnit!"

"No big deal. We'll just deny her reservation," Presley said matter-of-factly.

"And then she writes an article outing the whole place on a couple of rumors. Don't do that. Let me think, let me think," Krista said as much to herself as to Presley. "Do a background on this woman she wants to bring with her. Let's find out who she is."

Presley started tapping keys and Krista got up and walked around the yard. She paused at the back fence, lost in thought on how to handle this situation. The summer had been so perfect. She should've known this would happen and in the back of her mind she did. When things kept going smoothly she'd just pushed it so far back that it hadn't even occurred to her until now.

"I've got something," Presley said from the patio.

Krista walked over and waited.

"It looks like the woman is an escort, just as I expected."

Krista nodded and contemplated what to do next. "Do you still have contacts at the various pop culture sites?"

"Yep."

"Do you think you could find out Ms. Bell's routine? I want to talk to her face to face, but I don't want to set up a meeting. I don't want her to have time to prepare."

"You want to surprise her, but in a nonchalant way?"

"Exactly."

"Okay. Give me a few minutes to see what I can find."

Krista went in the house and refilled the water pitcher. *What was it with Brooke Bell and queer women,* she wondered. Her articles were always about women; nothing about gay or bisexual men. An idea was prickling at the back of her mind, but she couldn't bring it into focus just yet.

When she went back to the patio Presley was just ending a phone call.

"It just so happens that Brooke Bell starts her day at a little mom and pop diner. She stops in for a cup of coffee before she goes to wherever miserable homophobic people go to be mean."

"I guess I'll just happen to be there tomorrow and invite her to join me for a cup of…" Krista trailed off.

"A cup of what?"

"I'm not sure yet," she said, looking out over the canyon but seeing Brooke Bell's face instead. "Do a complete background check on Ms. Bell. I want to know all about her life before she came to the City of Angels," she said, turning toward Presley. "And I need it before I have coffee with her in the morning."

Presley nodded and her fingers quickly went to work.

5

Krista sat in a booth at the back of the diner. The huge windows that reached across the front gave her a great view of the street. She faced the door and would be able to easily see Brooke when she came in. The plan she'd come up with was risky, but if it worked, Lovers Landing should be secure. She took a deep breath in and slowly let it out. This very well could be the most important performance of her life.

She glanced down at her watch and, as if on cue, when she looked up Brooke Bell walked into the diner. Krista took a moment and was struck by the beauty of this woman. If she didn't know what a despicable person she was she'd be tempted to approach her in an entirely different manner. Brooke made her way to the counter where most of the stools were occupied with coffee drinkers.

Krista watched as the waitress behind the counter spoke to Brooke and then pointed in her direction. Brooke swung her head around and her bright blue eyes settled on the booth in the back. Krista gave her a little wave with what she hoped was an inviting smile.

Krista noticed the brightness in Brooke's eyes cooled as she recognized her. But she walked along the aisle toward Krista, obviously intrigued. Krista took that opportunity to enjoy Brooke's long stride and graceful arms as she came her way. When she realized what she was doing she attributed it to being around too many happy couples in Texas. Maybe it was time for her to have a little fun of her own, because there's no way she should be thinking about Brooke Bell this way. She made a mental note to look into finding a date for the fundraiser.

Brooke stopped at the table and looked down at Krista with a neutral expression.

"Care to join me?" Krista asked with a pleasant smile, pouring Brooke a cup of coffee from a carafe on the table.

Brooke narrowed her eyes and slid into the booth opposite Krista. They both took a sip from their cups.

"I'm not a big coffee drinker, but I have to say that this little diner makes a very good cup," Krista said warmly.

Brooke continued to stare.

Krista decided to sit back and wait. So she leaned against the back of the booth and gave Brooke another charming smile while she stared into those striking blue eyes. She knew the journalist wouldn't be able to stay quiet long.

"Why would you want to have coffee with me?" Brooke finally asked.

"I heard you were interested in my latest venture and I wanted to make sure you had the facts."

Brooke's eyebrows rose and she covered her surprise quickly, but not before Krista saw it.

"So it's true. You've opened a resort in Texas?" Brooke probed.

"It's more like a quaint lake getaway. Why? What did you hear?" Krista asked, taking another sip of her coffee. She watched Brooke and could see she was struggling with something. Then her face relaxed.

"You run a lake getaway," Brooke said, emphasizing Krista's words, "that is strictly for women, or should I say *queer* women."

Krista nodded and smiled. "If that's what you heard then surely you can see why I'm confused."

"I'm not understanding?" said Brooke.

"If you think this is a place for queer women then why would you want to come for a week?" Krista said, her tone turning serious.

Brooke sat back and smiled. "I figured you screened everyone beforehand. Do you also have a little meet and greet like this before you let them come to Texas?" she said, pointing between the two of them.

Krista smiled back, but what she really wanted to do was slap that smirk off this bitch's face.

Before Krista could respond Brooke said, "I guess that means I don't get to see Lovers Landing firsthand. What a shame." Brooke pouted and batted her eyes at Krista.

Deep breaths, deep breaths is what Krista said to herself over and over. Then she straightened her back and leaned forward with her best tempting smile. "I'd love for you to come see my little hideaway—as my guest," she said, challenging Brooke.

Brooke sat up abruptly and leaned back, obviously shocked. "What?"

"I'd like for you to be my guest," Krista said, knowing the first part of her plan was about to work. "But you have to come alone."

"Wait, what? I thought it was for couples?"

"Are you saying the woman that's coming with you is your girlfriend?"

"No!" Brooke exclaimed and then realized she had said that too loudly.

Krista sat back with her hands up palms out. "Whoa! I wasn't accusing you of anything."

Brooke sighed, exasperated. "Look Krista, I've heard things about this resort and wanted to do a story on it."

"A story? Do you mean come there and out the women you see, or out the resort as a place strictly for queer women?"

"I thought I'd decide the angle when I got there and saw it for myself."

Krista exhaled. "I see." She studied Brooke for several moments before she spoke. "I have a proposition for you."

Brooke raised her brows. "I'm listening."

"I would like for you to come to Texas with me. I'll personally show you around and what Lovers Landing offers. There is one condition."

"Of course there is. Let's hear it," Brooke said, annoyed.

"You have to go with an open mind. I'm going to show you everything and explain what it is we do."

Brooke's brow furrowed. "I'm not sure I understand."

"It's a special place and there's a reason I created it. I need you to have an open mind."

Brooke still looked confused.

"It's not just a place to take a woman and fuck. There's more to it than that," Krista said slyly.

Brooke bristled. "Damn, Krista," she whispered, looking around.

"Well, I know that's what you're thinking," she whispered back.

Brooke blew out a breath. "Okay. I'll keep an open mind."

Krista sat up and smiled. "Good. You'll get an email with an itinerary and instructions. I'll see you at the airport."

"You're flying with me?"

"Yep. You're all mine for a week, Brooke. Can you handle it?" Krista said, wanting to wink but deciding against it.

Brooke smirked, but Krista saw a flash of something cross her eyes.

* * *

Krista hit the button to call Julia. She sighed waiting for the call to connect, not wanting to share the news about the guest coming back with her.

"Are you missing me, Krissy?" Julia said, answering the phone.

"You have no idea."

"Shouldn't you be getting ready for the big shindig?"

"I'm about to. I wish you were here. I have a hot new stylist dressing me for tonight. You'd love it."

"What! I didn't think this was a big deal," Julia said, surprised.

"It's not really. The stylist and Presley have a little something going on, so she talked me into at least seeing what the woman can do. Turns out she's really good."

"How fun! Then I will be seeing photos from this event after all."

"I hope so for Serena's sake. She's the stylist. Have you been enjoying your time away from the lake?"

"Yes," Julia said, a note of suspicion in her voice.

"Oh good."

"What's going on, Krissy? I can tell something's not right."

Krista sighed. "Do you remember Brooke Bell?"

"Of course I do. Why?"

"She's coming to Lovers Landing with the next group."

"What! Why would she be coming here? Krista, what's going on?"

"She tried to make reservations with a fake name, but I figured it out."

"Holy shit!"

"I know! We can't tell her no because there's no telling what she'll write if we do."

"I understand that, but what are we going to do? Our guests trust us."

"I've got a plan."

"Okay, I'm listening."

"I met with her and told her I'd like to personally show her what our place is all about."

"Oh Krista, I don't know."

"I think something happened to her," Krista said softly.

"What do you mean?"

"Think about it, Jules. She seems to write only about bi and lesbian women. Presley is doing a deep dive into her background. If we don't find anything there then I'm hoping to show her that we're simply providing an outlet for discreet women."

"And if she doesn't see it that way?"

"Don't even say that, Jules. I'll find a way."

Julia was quiet for a moment. "What can I do to help?"

"If she sees you and Heidi in this twenty-five-year marriage living your happily ever after then maybe she'll soften."

"We'll do what we can. I mean, you're not really asking us to do anything other than be ourselves."

"I know. Heidi may need to be around for a few evenings when we do karaoke and movies. We'll figure it out."

"The girls are still here. This is their last week to work. Maybe it will help if she sees that we have two great daughters."

"I didn't think about that. Good idea," Krista said. "Courtney and Becca may have to tell Brooke how wonderful it is having two moms."

"What about the other guests? Will they get on the plane when they see her with you?"

"I've talked to two of the couples. They were at the lake in June and had so much fun they wanted to come back. The other couple is thinking it over. They are very careful so it's a bit of a risk for them. They're letting me know tomorrow."

"Damnit, everything was going so well." Julia sighed.

"I know. I expected this would happen eventually."

"All we can do is show her we're real people with families and lives that she probably wants, but for some reason can't have."

"I'm hoping we can show her that she doesn't have to ruin it for others for whatever reason she thinks she does."

"Okay. I'll get things ready here. You'd better get ready for your party. Have a good time. We can worry about this tomorrow."

"Right. I'll see you at the airport on Monday."

"Love ya, Krissy."

"Love you, too," Krista said, ending the call. A smile crept on her face. Julia had been her best friend forever and was always up for whatever she got them into. This was no different.

6

Krista walked into the venue with Presley and Serena not far behind. She had arranged for her assistant and stylist to accompany her at the fundraiser. After all, adding two to her table simply made more money for the LGBTQ+ youth initiative and that's what this was all about.

She walked the red carpet and paused at the step-and-repeat background for photos. The smile on her face was for Julia, knowing she would be looking for media coverage of the event. She turned and faced one way and then another and gave the photographers her best professional smile. Then she walked over to have a word with the announcers representing the fashion and entertainment outlets covering the event. She made sure everyone knew Serena was her stylist and an up and coming talent.

They found their table and Presley poured them all a glass of wine. Krista mingled with several acquaintances and people she knew in the industry until it was time for the program to start. After the short program a band began to play and the noise level in the room rose as the real party began.

Krista encouraged Presley and Serena to join the others on the dance floor. She watched and felt a pang of melancholy, trying to remember the last time she'd danced and held another woman close.

"Just who I want to see," Tara said, slipping into the seat next to Krista. "Are you remembering when we used to dance like that?" she asked, following Krista's gaze.

Krista's heart skipped a beat. Even after all these years Tara occupied a warm spot in her heart. There was no way they could be together again, but they were still dear friends.

"Come here," Tara said, scooting closer to Krista and pulling her into a hug. "See, we still fit," she said, pulling back with her eyebrows raised in a challenge.

Krista chuckled. "You seem to fit with that beautiful young woman I saw hanging on your arm earlier."

Tara ignored her comment and asked. "How's the lover's hideaway going?"

"It's going great. It's a shame there wasn't a place like this when we were together," Krista said, smiling at her ex.

"I still beat myself up sometimes that I couldn't be more patient," Tara said, a wistful look on her face.

"That was a long time ago and a different time, Tar." Krista leaned in and bumped shoulders with her friend.

"Yeah, but there are still folks hiding and look at you giving them a place to live their secrets."

Krista smiled at Tara, happy with that assessment. "You should bring your friend or some other friend out and see for yourself."

"Why don't I come out and spend the week with you? You know, for old times sake, as they say."

Krista rolled her eyes. "Because I'll be working. What do you think I do, lie on the beach all day?"

"I thought Julia was running things," Tara said, confused.

Krista chuckled. "She does, but I help her. We do it together."

Tara leaned in closer and lowered her voice. "Don't they stay in their cabins and have sex all day? I mean, what do you have to do?"

"There are lots of things to do. That's why they come. It's nice to walk around and be together without worrying about who's watching."

"Hmm, that does sound nice. Even though I'm out and don't really care, you know there's always someone looking when you don't know it." She found Krista's eyes and locked on them.

"What?" Krista asked after a few moments.

"I've missed you, Krissy." She held her hands up. "I know what you're thinking and I don't mean like that. I mean this." She pointed between the two of them. "We don't sit and visit, catch up. Why haven't we done that?"

"Because I've been in Texas for the summer and you've been busy with whoever is hanging on your arm at the moment."

"I should act hurt," she said, placing her hand over her heart, "but I know it's true. I get lonely. Don't you get lonely?"

"How could you be lonely, Tara? You're always dating someone."

"That's just it, Krista. It's dating. Don't you wish you had a partner?"

"Sometimes I do. Who knows, maybe one day I will."

"So if there's hope for you, do you think there's hope for me, too?"

Krista smiled affectionately. "If you'd give someone a chance, yes, there's hope for you, too."

"But tonight, I'm going to have to take that beautiful young woman home with me to chase away this loneliness. Unless I can entice you to come home with me instead," Tara said suggestively.

Krista thought about it for a moment. She and Tara had been good together and she had no doubts of what a fun night it would be. But she had a lake resort to save and would need to be at her sharpest beginning tomorrow.

"Come on," Tara begged. "I can see it in your eyes. You want to."

"Of course I want to. Why wouldn't I want to go home with *the* Tara Holloway? Just imagine the fun the tabloids would have with that." She laughed. "*But*," she emphasized, "I have to go back to Texas. I have an important week coming up."

"Okay," she said, sitting back in her chair with a sigh. "But I'm going to ask again when you're closed for winter. You do close in the winter, don't you?"

Krista tilted her head. "I don't know. We haven't gotten that far yet." They both laughed at the uncertainty.

"Give me a hug. I guess I'll go find my date and see if she can dance."

They hugged for a long moment and Tara left just as Presley and Serena made their way back to the table.

Presley looked at Krista with raised eyebrows.

"Don't even go there," she responded, holding up her hand.

When they sat back down Krista said, "I'm going to call it a night. You two stay and enjoy the party."

"Are you sure?" Presley asked.

"I am." She nodded. "Serena, thank you for tonight. I've had several people ask about my outfit so I'm sure you'll be getting calls. I felt very special tonight."

"Thank you so much for letting me dress you," Serena said, her eyes wide, clearly a fan.

"I'll talk to you tomorrow, Presley."

"I sent the latest information about the special guest. I found some interesting facts."

Krista nodded, hoping she'd found something to help this crazy plan of hers.

* * *

She carefully hung up her outfit and changed into her favorite comfy sweats and a tank top. A smile crossed her face as she thought back to her conversation with Tara. She often wondered why Tara wasn't in a long-term relationship. That's what she'd wanted all those years ago. She could still remember their arguments: "I want to go out in public with you just like any other couple." Tara went out plenty now, but most of the time it was with different women.

Krista grabbed her laptop and went out on the back porch. It was late, but still a warm night. Her thoughts moved from Tara to more pressing matters. She had learned several things about Brooke Bell in the last few days. Presley's detective work uncovered that Brooke grew up in Mississippi. Flashes from the Showtime documentary about growing up gay in that state made Krista wonder if it had touched Brooke's life in some way.

She had been married twice. Once when she was twenty and that lasted five years, then after she'd relocated to Los Angeles she married again at thirty, but that one only made it a couple of years. That was ten years ago. At forty-two, her dating life seemed non-existent or at least didn't make any kind of news because Presley's inquiries hadn't turned up anything.

There was no indication that she was particularly religious growing up. She had an older brother and a younger sister and her parents were still married. They seemed like the typical Southern family.

But for her to hunt facts that would obviously harm someone and then package them in a tell-all article that she knew would bring them harm and make money off of it made her a mystery to Krista. Why would someone do that? There had to be something that happened in her past to make her this callous and uncaring.

At least that's what Krista hoped. There were always people in the world that were only out for themselves and didn't care who they ran over or hurt to make their way to the top. Unfortunately, a large number of them were right here in Hollywood; however, most of the time something had happened in their lives to make them this way.

Krista thought about Brooke Bell, wondering what had happened to her; if she could somehow find out what changed her then maybe she could figure out a way to get her to leave Lovers Landing alone.

She read through the new information and looked at photos from Brooke's first marriage. *How did Presley find these family photos*, she wondered. Photos from her yearbook caught Krista's attention. As she looked through them she determined they must have been from her brother's senior year. That would've made Brooke a junior and her sister a freshman.

Krista studied the section that had random photos from

throughout the school year. Brooke's brother must have been one of the popular kids because she found him in many of the pictures. Brooke was in several shots with him and then others with her and, Krista guessed, a group of friends.

As the year progressed Brooke went from what appeared to be a smiling happy teenager to a sullen sad girl. In several of the photos of her brother's graduation she wasn't smiling. The group of friends that were in so many photos throughout the year were only in a few at the end of the year. Brooke wasn't smiling in these and one of the girls was missing.

"That's it!" Krista said, sitting up in her chair. She stared at the sad girl in the last photo. "What happened, Brooke? What did they do to you?"

She exhaled a loud breath and sat back in her chair remembering the weight of her teen years and hiding her confused feelings for other girls. When she and Julia realized they were struggling through the same things it was such a relief. It didn't necessarily ease the fear and pressure, but at least she wasn't alone.

She sat up and looked at the photo again. "Were you all alone, Brooke?" she whispered. "What did they do to you?"

7

Krista watched the car drive away and closed the front door. After pouring herself a glass of wine she went back out to the porch. She took a healthy swallow and sat back.

Allison Jennings and Libby Scott were so excited for their upcoming trip to Lovers Landing. To say they were surprised when Krista invited them over to share a bottle of wine wasn't quite accurate. They were more suspicious, but Krista had worked with them both and there was an element of trust between them.

She explained the addition of Brooke Bell to the guest list. It was Krista's turn to be surprised when they didn't immediately cancel the trip.

Allison and Libby had been together for almost twenty years, but only a chosen few knew this. Krista appreciated their diligence in keeping their relationship a secret all these years. She had no doubt it would have affected their careers because they both had been cast as Bond girls at one time, as well as in other roles as the beautiful leading lady.

They were taking a huge risk by going on this trip with a journalist that loved to out Hollywood's bisexual and lesbian women. Krista offered for them to attend at a later date, but this week fit in both their schedules and it would be months before they were both off at the same time again.

It was obvious to Krista that they really wanted to go on this trip. She shared with them what she was trying to accomplish and how she planned to do it. They looked at one another and decided to come along anyway.

Krista dearly hoped she could get Brooke to open up to her—if not to save Lovers Landing, then to protect Allison and Libby. But what about Brooke? Surely writing these articles didn't give her happiness. Perhaps there was another reason; maybe Brooke Bell needed saving and didn't know it.

* * *

At the airport Krista checked in with the pilot and attendant. Everything was ready to whisk this week's group away to their lake retreat at Lovers Landing. Her heart thumped in her chest as she waited for the couples to arrive. Usually she wasn't nervous, just excited to begin the trip. She truly enjoyed welcoming and entertaining these women. Their secrets and whys weren't important to her. The chance to let them relax and be themselves was what mattered, but this week was different. She took a deep breath and exhaled, knowing Julia was waiting on her end ready to welcome them. She smiled, because Julia could certainly be charming with her Texas drawl and down home hospitality. She was still smiling when two cars arrived. *Here we go*, she thought.

First to arrive were Anna Cain and Shelley Haskell. They were both producers and had been dating about a year. Anna had worked with Krista on her last sitcom and when Krista approached her about Lovers Landing she was quick to book a week in June. They had such a good time and were looking forward to their return trip.

Next were Renee Oliver and Megan Easterling. Krista greeted them and was looking forward to hearing about Megan's next project. She was a highly sought after director and planned to shoot a romantic comedy with several A-list stars. One of the couples featured in the movie was gay and there had been notable buzz already. Renee was Megan's longtime girlfriend. They were both out and just wanted to get away before filming began. Lovers Landing provided the seclusion they wanted.

Both couples had been told Brooke Bell would be joining them and opted to come to Lovers Landing anyway. Anna and Shelley were discreet about their relationship, but didn't consider themselves important enough to warrant an article. Renee and Megan simply didn't care. They figured they were old news anyway.

Brooke was next to drive up. Even though Krista's heart accelerated she flashed her a relaxed, welcoming smile she'd practiced for years. She introduced Brooke to the others and invited all of them to board the plane.

The attendant showed them to their seats as the last car pulled up. Krista touched Brooke's elbow, causing her to stop just as she started to walk up the steps to the plane. "I'd like to introduce you to the last of my guests."

Brooke turned around and her mouth dropped momentarily when she saw Allison Jennings and Libby Scott get out of the car.

Krista noticed her reaction and smiled to herself as she walked past her and greeted Allison and Libby. "Welcome, ladies. I'm so glad you're joining me this week at Lovers Landing," Krista said, turning on the charm.

While their driver retrieved their bags from the trunk of the car Krista walked them to the stairs. "I'd like you to meet Brooke Bell," Krista said with a smile. "Brooke, this is Allison Jennings and Libby Scott."

"It's so nice to meet you," Libby said, holding out her hand.

Krista thought she saw a flicker of surprise before Brooke took her hand. "It's nice to meet you."

"Hi Brooke," Allison said with a genuine smile.

"It's nice to meet you, Allison."

"Shall we board, ladies?" Krista suggested. "We have refreshments waiting."

The four women climbed the steps and the attendant showed

them to their seats. Brooke sat in the back with Krista. After everyone had their drinks and the pilot readied the plane, Krista walked to the front.

"I'll be in the back if anyone needs anything or has any questions. This is Hillary," Krista said, nodding to the attendant standing beside her. "She'll get you refills once we're in the air. If you need anything don't hesitate to ask her or me. Your week of sun, fun, and pleasure begins now. Let's go to Lovers Landing."

The group clapped and she walked back to her seat next to Brooke. She sat down, leaned over and said quietly, "Honestly, I'm a bit nervous."

"Really?" Brooke asked, surprised. "Your smile didn't look nervous."

"That's from years of tamping down the jitters and smiling through it."

Brooke looked at her curiously. "You expect me to believe that?"

"Why wouldn't you?" Krista looked over at her.

Brooke dropped her head and raised her eyebrows.

"You don't think I get nervous? I do. I want everyone to have a good time; it's my responsibility."

Brooke's face softened. "Okay."

"I know I asked you to keep an open mind, but you do realize you're going on vacation."

"No I'm not!"

"Yeah you are. You're aren't paying for any of this. You're not on assignment. You may be collecting information for a project, but I want you to have a good time. When's the last time you were on vacation?"

Brooke paused and finally said, "I can't remember."

"Well then, please relax and let me show you a good time. It's important to me. Okay?" Krista gave her the million dollar smile that had won her several Emmys.

Before Brooke could say anything the pilot asked them to secure their seat belts as they taxied to the runway.

Krista was determined to get this woman to relax. She looked over at her and smiled as the plane sped down the runway. Then she grabbed Brooke's hand and squeezed until the plane was in the air and leveled off.

"Sorry," she said quietly. "Takeoffs scare me."

"No problem," Brooke said with a small smile.

Krista smiled back and their eyes locked. *What beautiful blue eyes*, Krista thought.

* * *

They taxied to the hangar and Krista looked out the window, spotting Julia waiting with the van. She waved and relaxed just a tad. Surely they could pull this off; if not, at least they were going down together.

She turned to Brooke. "I have to go up front and take care of a few things. Will you be okay?"

Brooke nodded. "Of course. I think I can get off a plane by myself."

Krista arched an eyebrow. "We've got to work on that attitude." She leaned down and whispered in her ear, "Remember, you're on vacation."

Brooke scoffed, but not before Krista saw the smile playing at the corners of her mouth.

"Welcome to Texas," Krista said from the front of the plane. "It will take us a few minutes to load the van. There's no rush. When you gather your things, watch your step and make your way outside."

She walked down the steps and called, "Hey!"

Julia peeked around from the back of the van where she was supervising. She grinned and gave Krista a hug.

"Thanks, I needed that." Krista smiled back.

"Is it that bad?" Julia said, stressed.

"No. So far so good. But that is one uptight woman. I'm going to have to show her how to relax."

Julia chuckled. "You're the perfect teacher."

Krista smirked as Julia walked past her to help the ladies board the van.

When everyone was inside she turned to Krista. "You didn't tell me she was such a beautiful woman."

"I know!" Krista sighed and stepped in the van. "This is Julia," Krista said, introducing her. "We have been best friends since…" She turned to Julia.

Before she could finish Julia said, "Forever. It's been forever."

The ladies laughed at her feigned exasperated tone.

"I have refreshments for you. We call this Lovers Landing Licker, spelled l-i-c-k-e-r," she said, spelling it out. The ladies chuckled as she passed out the drinks.

"It's actually a tropical cocktail that we both love. We make ours without the booze so we can drink it all day long," Krista explained. "This batch has a little vodka in it especially for you," she said, looking at each guest. She paused for a moment when she met Brooke's eyes.

"Sit back and enjoy the ride. It'll take us about an hour to get to the lake. I'd point out any interesting things on the way, but let's be honest. You don't care! We just want to get to the lake and laze on the beach," Julia said, buckling in and starting the van.

"Do you mind if I sit here?" Krista asked Brooke, sitting down beside her.

"It's your party," she said with no emotion.

Krista ignored her lack of enthusiasm and asked, "What do you think? Do you like it?"

Brooke took a sip of the drink and her eyes widened. "This is good!"

Krista laughed. "You act surprised. I don't know what you expect, Brooke, but I honestly want you to have a good time. That's the goal for everyone on this bus."

Brooke looked at her skeptically.

Krista sighed. "Will you at least try?"

Brooke's expression was guarded. "It's hard for me to relax. I feel like I always have to be on, if you know what I mean. There's always a story right in front of me if I see it and dare to write it."

Krista nodded, considering her words. "Look, you know what the story is this week. Or at least you think you do. So shut down work mode; the story will still be there. Let me show you a good time. Relax and enjoy yourself. You can worry about the story later in the week. Deal?" Krista held out her hand.

Brooke narrowed her eyes. "You are a charmer, Krista Kyle. I already knew that, but okay. I'll try," Brooke said, taking Krista's hand. She was rewarded with Krista's best smile.

8

An hour later they pulled onto a one lane paved road that turned into a gravel parking lot. The van stopped next to the deck attached to the back of the restaurant and bar.

"Right this way," Julia said, leading them off the van.

There were four golf carts and two younger women waiting. Once everyone was off the van, Krista turned to the group.

"Welcome to Lovers Landing," she said, holding her arms out wide. "I'd like for you to meet Courtney and Becca." Krista smiled at the young women. "They're Julia's daughters and my god-daughters. This really is a family owned and family run affair. You'll meet their other mom, Heidi, at some point this week."

"Courtney will escort Anna and Shelley," Julia said. "Renee and Megan, Becca will drive you to your cabin." Then she turned to Allison and Libby with a smile. "I'll take care of you."

"Brooke is with me." Krista grinned. "We will answer any questions and show you around the property. There's a map and list of things to do in your cabin. The restaurant behind us is always open or we can deliver to your cabin. This is your week to do as you please. If you need anything please do not hesitate to ask. We want this to be the best week of your lives."

"Thanks, Krista," Shelley said. "We had the best week back in June and I'm sure this one will be too."

"Oh, I'm glad."

"I do hope there will be another karaoke night with dancing," Anna said, grinning at Shelley.

"Oh yeah." Courtney laughed. "Those are the best!"

"Any questions?" Julia asked, looking around. "Oh, one other thing. You don't have to do anything while you're here. Those cabins and the area around them are pretty wonderful by themselves, so if you want to hibernate we can make sure no one bothers you."

"Okay, let's go," Krista said, grabbing her bag and putting it in the back of the golf cart.

She reached for Brooke's but when Brooke realized what Krista was doing she grasped the handle first. Krista's hand grabbed Brooke's hand along with the handle. "Oh, sorry," she said, pulling her hand away.

"You don't have to do everything," Brooke said, shrugging.

"I kind of do." Krista put her hand back over Brooke's and took the bag. She gave her a smile full of sweetness. "It's my job."

Brooke smiled cautiously and let her take the bag. Krista put it on the back of the golf cart, counting Brooke's smile as a small victory.

She drove them down by the beach and the walkway to the dock, watching Brooke out of the corner of her eye. How anyone wouldn't find this beautiful was beyond her. She slowed down for a moment to look out over the water.

"I love it here," she said softly. "Everything is slow and easy. You don't have to worry about someone taking a photo and posting it. You can be yourself." She looked over at Brooke. "I saw the surprise on your face when Allison and Libby got out of their car. Did you know that they've been together for twenty years?"

Brooke's eyebrows rose in shock.

"There is no way they would have been cast as James Bond's girlfriend if they were open with their relationship."

"Or those rom-coms they were in after that," Brooke said, still surprised.

"Can you imagine anyone else in those roles?"

Brooke swung her head around to face Krista. "No!"

Krista nods. "That's why they wanted to come here, Brooke. They can be themselves and know their secret is safe."

Krista didn't wait for her to respond before she started them moving again. They drove the rest of the way to Brooke's cabin in silence.

Brooke got out of the cart and spun around, gaping at the landscape. In one direction was a private beach just steps away. It stretched out to meet the water and they could hear the gentle waves. There was a covered porch and just beyond that was a fire pit with two chairs arranged to view the lake. Trees surrounded the cabin, giving it a natural privacy fence. The smell of fresh air wafted off the water and rustled the leaves in the trees beyond the house.

Krista was pleased with Brooke's response. Maybe the rigid journalist was beginning to loosen up a little.

She wondered if Brooke had noticed that so far her fellow travelers were not only polite, but friendly to her on this risky journey. Even Krista was surprised when Libby had come to the back of the plane and visited for a time during the flight.

"This is incredible," Brooke said breathlessly, obviously enthralled.

"Are you beginning to see why I like it here so much?"

"I do," Brooke answered, still looking out over the water.

Krista took a moment to study her profile. Her blonde hair rested behind her ear. A perfect ear, Krista noticed, with a lobe aching to be nibbled. Her nose was rounded at the end and she remembered it wrinkled a little when she genuinely smiled. But those blue eyes were what intrigued Krista. They could be ice cold and guarded and just as quickly turn clear and sparkling. She couldn't help but wonder what color they were when full of desire.

What the fuck! Krista shook her head, bringing her thoughts back to her mission. *Where did that come from*, she wondered. Surely it was this beautiful backdrop combined with a stunning woman. It was good to know Krista still had a fire inside her, even if it was smoldering with the wrong woman. When this was over she'd have to do something about that. In the meantime, she knew her cheeks were flaming with her thoughts. She doubted Brooke would notice.

"If you look through the trees this way," Krista said, walking toward the water, drawing Brooke's eyes past the cabin.

"I see another cabin," Brooke said.

"Right. That's mine."

Brooke looked at her then and tilted her head. "Are you all right? Your cheeks are red."

"I'm fine. Anyway," she said, nodding toward her cabin. "If you need anything, I'm right there."

Brooke looked at her strangely, but Krista kept talking. "We usually don't have guests in this one. Julia lives in town, but when she stays over this is hers. We had this one and mine decorated just for us because–" Krista stopped herself. "I'm rambling, sorry about that."

Brooke grinned and Krista saw that little wrinkle on her nose. "It's okay, Krista. I know you are a wonderful actor, but I can see you're nervous again."

Krista looked down and chuckled. "I told you! Now do you believe me?"

Brooke laughed. "You do understand why it's hard to believe you, right?"

"What do you mean?" Krista asked.

"I know you're trying to keep me from writing about this secret hideaway, so you'll say anything."

Krista leaned back as if Brooke had struck her. "No I won't! I'm telling you the truth. I'm showing you exactly who we are."

"I didn't mean to offend you, but surely you know how hard it is to trust anyone in Hollywood."

Krista sighed. "I get that, but I'm not just anyone, Brooke."

Brooke held her gaze. "Okay. I can see that. I'm sorry."

Krista tried to smile. "I'm not trying to deceive you. I want you to understand why Julia and I started this place and what it means to the people that come here. Now, let me show you inside." Krista walked away, needing for this conversation to be over.

She grabbed Brooke's bag from the golf cart and they walked into the cabin. She showed her around and left her bag on the chest in the bedroom.

"I'm going to my cabin and change clothes. Would you like to walk along the beach before dinner?" Krista asked.

"That sounds nice."

Krista smiled to herself at the noticeable softening in Brooke's tone. "Okay, I'll be back shortly."

Brooke followed her onto the porch and watched her drive to her cabin and then went back inside.

* * *

Krista threw her bag on the bed and found her favorite pair of denim shorts in her dresser. She threw on a tank top and slipped into comfortable sandals. After changing she took a moment and looked out at the water from her bedroom window. Today she'd learned that Brooke Bell was one tightly wound woman. She was a bit stubborn, but there were moments when she loosened up.

Krista walked onto the back porch and sat in her rocking chair. She needed a few moments of calm to figure out what was going on with her. It was her bright idea to bring Brooke here and show her what Lovers Landing was all about and what it meant to them. She wasn't supposed to notice how bright Brooke's blue eyes were when she smiled. Or the little wrinkle between her brows when she was being stubborn. And what about the spark that shot up her arm when she'd accidentally put her hand over Brooke's on her bag.

All of this was not only unexpected, but shocking. There is no way she could be attracted to someone like Brooke Bell. She shook her head to free those irresponsible thoughts. Her job was to keep Brooke from telling their secrets, not seduce her into what could only end in disaster.

Enough of that. She inhaled a deep breath, let it out and hopped out of her chair. She walked over to Brooke's cabin and found her sitting in one of the chairs at the fire pit.

"You look relaxed," Brooke said.

Krista could feel Brooke's eyes roaming up and down her body until they settled on her own blue ones. It suddenly occurred to Krista that they both had blue eyes. Brooke looked just as confused as Krista felt. "Are you enjoying the view?"

"It is so peaceful out here," Brooke said, looking away.

Krista followed her gaze. "If you sit here quietly you can see and hear the waves lapping onto the beach. It'll put you to sleep."

"It'll make you forget your troubles, too."

"What troubles do you have?" Krista asked. "I thought I was the one with troubles," she said, sitting in the chair next to her.

"I'm your trouble, aren't I?" Brooke asked honestly.

Krista looked over at her. "I don't know yet. Are you trouble, Brooke Bell?"

Their eyes locked and neither said anything. Finally Krista got up. "Come on, let's walk to the beach and down to the dock."

They walked along in comfortable silence. In the distance they could hear the hum of boats on the lake and an occasional burst of laughter followed by a splash.

"It feels good to walk after traveling most of the day," Krista commented.

"Are you one of those people that workout every day?" Brooke asked with a hint of judgement in her voice.

Krista chuckled. "Not even close. I like to walk and swim and play. My favorite workout is sitting on that deck up by the restaurant or on my back porch looking out at the water with a drink in my hand."

Brooke made an approving hum. "I'd sign up for that."

"Consider it done. You are invited for coffee on my back porch in the morning."

"What if I don't drink coffee?" Brooke asked lightly.

Krista cut her head sideways. "You expect me to believe that? Any respected journalist that works on a deadline mainlines coffee. Besides, I met you in a coffee shop."

Brooke laughed. "Guilty as charged. Except I'm not so sure about the respected part."

Before Krista could comment she heard her name being called from the dock. Courtney and Becca were at the end of the dock waving at her and pointing at the boat.

"I guess we'd better see what's going on," Krista said, leading them down the walkway.

"Aunt Krissy, look who's in the boat!" Becca exclaimed, pointing.

"Sappho, what are you doing in there?" Krista asked playfully.

"I thought cats didn't like water," Brooke said.

"This one does," Krista said. "Did your mom not tell you about the boat ride she went on with us?"

"No! When?" Courtney asked.

"On the last break between groups. I think y'all had gone to see your friends in Austin. We took the boat over to the Cliffs to swim. We're zooming along and I look down and there's Sappho rolling around on the floor between the skis."

"Come on silly girl," Becca said, jumping in the boat and cuddling the cat. "We're through cleaning up down here. We'll see you at dinner." She got out of the boat and she and Courtney began to walk towards shore.

Courtney turned around. "I hope you have a good time, Ms. Bell. Bye, Aunt Krissy."

"Bye girls," Krissy said, giving them a little wave.

"Aunt Krissy, huh," Brooke teased.

"Yep, that's me."

"Do they know why I'm here?"

"I'm not sure. Julia may have told them," Krista said, wrinkling her forehead. "Courtney takes her job very seriously. She wants to be sure everyone is having a good time."

Brooke watched them walk away. "You and Julia have been friends since you were their age?"

"Even younger. Kindergarten. When we were in high school we both worked here."

"So that's one reason you wanted to buy it?"

"Kind of. I can remember the summer that I finally accepted that I was different. I mean, as if high school isn't hard enough, then you realize you like girls instead of boys and go through the denial and everything else. Let's walk to the beach," Krista said, leading them back up the walkway. "As I was saying, I remember that summer my friends would come out and spend the day on the beach. The guys would be watching the girls and there I was watching the girls right along with them. One day I caught Julia ogling the same girl I was and then we both knew."

"I thought you were best friends!"

"We were, we are. But we'd both been too scared to actually say it out loud." Krista laughed. "I can still remember how frightening that was and now I'm laughing."

"Were the two of you together then?"

Krista stopped and looked at Brooke, astonished. "What? No! Julia and I have never been together."

"Oh, sorry. I just thought, since you were best friends and both liked girls..." Her voice trailed off.

"We were the only lesbians in our school that we knew of, but we never felt like that. I'd take a bullet for Julia, but I've never been in love with her or seen her like that. She's always been my dear friend. Did you have any lesbians in high school? Where did you grow up?" Krista asked, knowing but wanting to see if Brooke would share.

"Uh, I grew up in Mississippi. There were a couple of girls in my school."

"Mississippi, another gay friendly state," Krista said sarcastically. They'd stopped at two adirondack chairs facing the beach and Krista sat.

"Yeah," Brooke said, sitting next to her. "There was a girl that kind of got caught in our school."

"What do you mean?" asked Krista.

"Well, I think these two girls were together and then somehow one of the 'popular' boys found out," Brooke said, using air quotes.

"What happened?"

"If I remember right, the boy told one of the girls if she didn't drop her girlfriend then he'd tell the whole school."

"But the school found out anyway?" Krista asked. She knew that

Brooke had to be talking about the girl that disappeared from the yearbook photos.

"No, the boy didn't tell. The girls weren't friends anymore. One of them acted like nothing happened and the other kind of faded away. I don't know if she left school or what. It was all rumors at the time."

"That's terrible. I feel bad for both girls," Krista said, staring at the sand. She had a feeling one of the girls was Brooke and that made her sad. Could this have been the beginning of Brooke's bitterness for gay women?

"You feel bad? Why?"

Krista looked over at Brooke, her brow furrowed. "Don't you? Someone forced those two girls out of their friendship. It's hard to be brave anytime, but don't you remember how hard high school was? Or at least it was for me."

"High school was hard for you?"

"Yes! I wanted to fit in and had a wonderful group of friends, but I was also afraid if they found out about me that they'd drop me. Was it like that for you?"

Brooke thought for a moment before speaking. "I went to a small high school. Everyone knew everyone so it was hard to have a secret."

"I guess those two girls did until they didn't. How did you find out about them?"

Brooke's eyes widened as if she'd been caught. "I didn't. Like I said, it was a rumor."

Krista knew Brooke was lying. She was the girl that acted like nothing happened and the other girl that faded away was the one missing from the photos. Just as she'd suspected, Brooke Bell had been hurt because of a woman. Now all Krista had to do was figure out a way to heal this wound that had festered for over twenty years. Lovers Landing depended on it.

Krista stood up and reached her hand out to Brooke. "Enough sad talk. Let's have dinner."

Brooke looked at Krista's hand for a moment before she took it and then gazed into Krista's eyes.

Krista smiled and didn't drop her hand until they'd taken a few steps.

9

When they walked into the restaurant Julia, Heidi, and the girls were at one table and over by the window overlooking the lake were Anna and Shelley. Krista watched Brooke take in the room. Her eyes darkened a moment when she noticed Anna and Shelley holding hands.

"Let's go say hi to Julia. I want you to meet her wife," Krista said, walking away.

"Join us," Julia said as they walked over.

"Brooke, I'd like you to meet Heidi Lansing," Krista said, introducing her. Heidi stood up and held out her hand. Brooke shook it as Krista continued, "Heidi is Jules's wife and where these girls got their smarts."

"Thanks a lot," Julia said.

"Darlin', you know they got their charm and beauty from you," Krista said soothingly.

Both girls laughed. "Damn, we're something!"

"You certainly are and don't ever forget it!" Krista said, putting an arm around each of them.

"Do you work here, too?" Brooke asked.

"No," Heidi chuckled.

"She's our legal department," Krista said. "Her law practice is in town, but she helps out when we need it."

"Actually, I'm here tonight because the chef is preparing scallops," Heidi said, widening her eyes.

"Do you like scallops?" Krista asked Brooke. "She makes the best I've ever eaten."

"I do like them."

"Would you order for us, Julia? I want to show her the deck."

"Sure thing. What would you like to drink?"

Krista smirked. "You know what I want. Bring me a Lovers Landing licker."

The girls giggled and shook their heads. "I can't believe you call it that," Courtney said.

"I'll have the same," Brooke said boldly.

Krista looked at her and raised her brows. "I may get you to relax after all."

Brooke gave her a smirk and half smile.

"We'll be back in a few minutes," Krista said.

She took them through the back door that led out on the deck.

"Let's sit for a minute," she said, choosing chairs that had an unobstructed view of the lake.

"I can see why you like it here so much," Brooke said softly.

"Wait a couple of hours when it's really dark. The stars are brilliant."

They sat for a moment and then Krista said, "I'm sure you noticed Anna and Shelley holding hands. Can you imagine them doing that in LA? There would already be pictures posted on every social media site. That's what's appealing about coming here, Brooke. It's little things like holding hands."

They heard footsteps crunching on gravel and then, "Hey Krista!" Megan hollered.

"Hi," Krista waved as they walked up on the deck.

"Renee and I want to try paddle boarding tomorrow. Could you teach us?"

"Sure!" She turned to Brooke. "I'll teach you, too." Then she turned back to Meagan and Renee. "It's really easy, you'll pick it right up."

"It looks like fun," said Renee.

"For me, it's calming," Krista replied. "You'll see."

"See you tomorrow. We're hungry!" Megan said as they walked into the restaurant.

When they'd gone inside Brooke turned to Krista. "I saw them holding hands too."

Krista chuckled as she stood. "Have you tried it? It's nice."

She started toward the door and Brooke quickly passed her and stopped before going inside. "I get what you're doing here, Krista. Romance is on full display."

"I'm glad you see that. When's the last time you were romanced?" Krista asked, not sure where the question came from.

"When's the last time you were?" Brooke threw the question right back at her.

Krista took a deep breath, thinking about it. "It's been a very long time," she said, exhaling.

"Same here," Brooke said, holding the door open for them.

"It's been a long time since I've *wanted* to romance anyone either," Krista said, making eye contact and then walking by. She could feel Brooke's eyes on her as they walked to their table.

Dinner was lively and fun with Courtney and Becca entertaining the table.

In between bouts of laughter Brooke told Krista, "You were right. Dinner was incredible."

"I'm so glad you enjoyed it."

"Do you think you can handle things from here?" Julia asked Krista.

"Why? Are you ready to go home?" Krista teased. "It's time for a secret lesbian lovefest. I promised Brooke!"

Courtney and Becca looked at one another wide eyed. To Brooke's credit she remained stoic.

Heidi and Julia burst out laughing, pointing at their daughters. "You should see your faces!"

"We knew you were kidding," Becca said quickly.

"Yeah we did," chirped Courtney.

"You so didn't!" Krista said, getting up and squeezing Becca's shoulders.

Courtney laughed. "Okay, you got us! What else is new! We never know because you and Mom have done some crazy shit."

Krista and Julia looked at one another and shrugged.

"Come on girls," Heidi said. "Let's go home before they embarrass you again."

"I'll see you in the morning," Julia said to Krista. "See you tomorrow, Brooke."

"Bye Julia, thanks for sharing your family this evening."

Julia tilted her head. "Anytime."

"Let me check in with the kitchen. I'll just be a minute," Krista said to Brooke as she got ready to leave.

When she came back Brooke was gazing out the back window.

"Ready to go?"

Brooke nodded and they walked out the back door.

"Thanks for going along with that ruse on the girls. I'm surprised they believed me."

"It surprised me too," Brooke chuckled. Krista loved the deep little laugh that echoed into the night. "I wasn't sure you didn't mean it," she added.

Krista looked over at her and could see such a difference from this morning. Her expression was carefree and her blonde hair shimmered in the moonlight. When she'd met Brooke in the diner that day she had a striking severe, yet stunning beauty. But tonight she was ethereal. Her visage begged to be touched and Krista had to stop herself from reaching out and doing just that. She'd fallen behind a step as she admired this change in Brooke. Either way the woman was exquisite and Krista was stunned at this admission.

"You okay?" Brooke asked, turning slightly.

Krista was thankful for the darkness, so Brooke couldn't see her eyes. She was afraid it would be obvious what she was thinking. "Just enjoying the walk," she said quietly.

"Should we be holding hands?" Brooke said.

"What?" Krista said, swinging her head around.

Brooke chuckled. "I thought it was why people come here. Isn't that what you said?"

Krista laughed. "I did say that, but you know what I meant. Why? Do you want to hold my hand?" Krista decided to challenge her.

"I want to walk out to the water," she said as her cabin came into view.

"Let's go," Krista said, brushing her hand against Brooke's and linking their pinkies for a moment.

Brooke didn't pull her hand away and neither said anything as they continued to amble along.

Krista dropped Brooke's hand and stepped out of her sandals as they reached the water. She stepped in ankle deep and turned to Brooke. "Join me? It's quite nice."

Brooke eyed her and then stepped out of her own sandals and stepped into the water. Her eyes widened and her face visibly softened. "This is wonderful." She paused. "So soothing."

Krista smiled, pleased. "It is," she whispered.

Brooke looked out over the water. "Krista, I know we're not friends and why you're doing this, but thank you for today. It's been really nice."

"You don't know me and I don't know you, Brooke. But that doesn't mean I don't want to," Krista said with a delicate smile. She stepped out of the water and back into her sandals. "Don't forget you're invited for coffee in the morning. I'll warn you though, it won't be early."

"You're not an early riser?" Brooke said, reaching down for her sandals.

"No! I had to get up early and be on set for years. I love to sleep in."

"But what if I want to see the sunrise?" Brooke asked.

"By all means, feel free. I can't wait for you to tell me all about it."

Brooke laughed. "I won't be up early either."

Krista chuckled. "I'll text you when the coffee is ready. We can plan our day." She looked out into the darkening night. "Do you need me to walk you in?"

"No, I'll be fine. Thanks."

"Night, Brooke." Krista took a few steps toward her cabin and then turned to face Brooke. "Just so you know, I had a good time today, too."

Brooke nodded and Krista walked away.

Krista stepped up onto her porch. So many thoughts were playing in her head. Brooke had finally begun to relax and Krista really liked this person she was getting to know. She couldn't help but wonder if Brooke thought the same about her.

10

The next morning Krista got ready for the day and then made coffee. She texted Brooke and couldn't help smiling. She hoped to get to know Brooke better today. Yesterday had been surprising and enlightening. She was sure something had happened to Brooke in high school and had a feeling she was one of the two girls from her story.

She looked out and could see Brooke walking over from her cabin. Her head was down and her shoulders sagged. This wasn't the same woman she'd said goodnight to a few hours earlier.

Krista opened the door and greeted her. "Good morning," she said cheerily.

"Morning," Brooke mumbled without making eye contact.

"Come in, the coffee is ready," Krista smiled and walked to the counter to pour Brooke a mug. "I have fallen in love with this vanilla creamer, but I have a couple of other choices and sugar if that's how you take it." Krista stepped out of the way and watched Brooke as she poured the vanilla creamer into her cup. She stirred it and tasted it, but didn't say anything.

Krista had a sinking feeling in her stomach. Something wasn't right. "Are you okay? Did you sleep all right?"

"I slept great," Brooke said, her words clipped. "After I got used to the quiet."

"It is quiet out here. I think of it as peaceful. It gives you a chance to think."

"Sometimes thinking isn't the best thing to do though," Brooke said cryptically.

Krista furrowed her brow. "Am I giving you things to think about that unsettle you?" When Brooke simply stared, not answering, Krista added, "Then that's a good thing."

"How so?"

"Let me ask you a question, Brooke. Does it make you feel good or successful when you publish a piece that is obviously going to change someone's life? Change it in a way that they didn't necessarily want?"

Brooke narrowed her eyes and waited a few moments before responding. "I don't feel good about hurting people. Did you ever think I'm trying to help them?"

Krista leaned back with surprise. "Help them. How does telling someone's secrets help them?"

"The articles I've written haven't ended anyone's life. It helped some of them live their lives openly."

Krista couldn't believe what she was hearing. "You're trying to justify what you did by thinking you helped them? It was their story to tell, Brooke. Not yours."

"I guess we don't see it the same way."

"I guess not," Krista said, walking over to the door and looking out. She was going to have to think about this. Brooke thought she was helping these women. What a fucked up view. She sighed and turned around. "Let's go have breakfast," she said with a forced smile. "I promised to teach Megan and Renee to paddle board."

"Thanks for the coffee," Brooke said, following Krista outside to the golf cart.

They rode to the restaurant in silence and walked inside. "Choose a table and I'll be right with you," Krista said to Brooke. She needed a minute to process this changed attitude in Brooke. It was like she'd reverted back to the rigid woman she'd met in the diner.

She walked over to where Allison and Libby were having breakfast. "Good morning," she said warmly.

"Good morning to you." Allison smiled. "How are things going with our sapphic chatterbox?"

Krista sighed. "I'm not sure. Yesterday, as the day went on, she relaxed and became a different person. But this morning she's back to business and looking for a scandal."

"If anyone can make her understand this situation," Libby said, swinging her hand in an arc, "it's you."

"Thanks. I appreciate your confidence in me, but it would break my heart if she wrote something that hurt you," Krista said, looking from one to the other.

"Darling," Allison said with a dramatic accent. "We've weathered plenty of storms in this crazy business we love. We will certainly make it through this one." She reached over and took Libby's hand in hers. "Right, babe?"

"That's right." Libby smiled affectionately.

"Is there anything special you want to do today? After breakfast we're doing a little paddle boarding and this afternoon we're taking a boat ride if you're interested."

"As lovely as those sound we have found that our porch looks out over the most tranquil little inlet. We shared coffee this morning with a couple of deer and it was enchanting." Allison beamed.

Libby leaned in and lowered her voice. "That four post bed is terribly nice too."

Krista chuckled. "I couldn't agree more," she said softly. "Let us know if you need anything though," she added, standing up.

"We will."

She went to the table where Brooke was studying the menu and sat across from her.

"They look content, but I don't notice them holding hands," Brooke pointed out, a hint of snark in her voice.

Krista studied her for a moment and shook her head, stopping the nasty remark she wanted to make. Ignoring Brooke's comment, she put on one of her best smiles. "Let's have breakfast and then we'll do some paddle boarding." Her eyes locked on Brooke's and she tilted her head. "Maybe we can find that pleasant relaxed woman that I had dinner with last night. I so enjoyed her company."

Brooke's mouth fell open and before she could say anything their server appeared.

Krista could feel Brooke's eyes boring into her as she ordered. She wasn't sure if Brooke was challenging her or herself. Either way, Krista was determined to hear this woman laugh today.

They quickly ate breakfast and Krista drove them back to their cabins to change into their swimming suits. She texted Megan and Renee to meet them at the beach.

Then she took a couple of calming breaths and thought about Brooke Bell. What could make her change back into the stoic journalist overnight? They had such a nice day yesterday—then it struck her. Maybe Brooke was afraid. Krista knew Brooke had a good time, too. But opening up about her high school days made her vulnerable and that was something she was sure Brooke Bell never showed.

Well, Krista thought, skimming over the water on a paddle board had always been calming for her. She hoped it would do the same for Brooke because she had to break down the wall that she'd built overnight and let that beautiful likeable woman out.

She walked to the golf cart and stopped at Brooke's cabin. When Brooke came out Krista almost lost her breath. She was wearing a red high cut one piece swimsuit that accentuated her long legs. Over it she wore a see through cover up that just added to the allure.

Krista bit down on her bottom lip and couldn't stop herself. "Wow, Ms. Bell, you look..." Krista couldn't find the words when Brooke's eyes met hers. She saw a spark flash in those clear blue orbs and then Brooke looked away.

Krista gathered herself. "You look amazing. Now what were you saying yesterday about working out?"

Brooke blushed. "Nothing. You were telling me about your favorite workouts."

Krista chuckled. "I think you're holding out on me."

"I run. It helps me clear my head and get my thoughts together when I'm working on a big piece."

"I hope you'll like paddle boarding then. It's not as strenuous, but it is freeing." Krista mashed the accelerator and drove them to the beach.

Megan and Renee were already in the water, splashing and laughing with one another. Courtney had four paddle boards on the beach waiting for them.

They got out of the golf cart and Brooke said quickly, "You wear that swimsuit well yourself, Krista Kyle."

Krista stopped and turned around to meet Brooke's eyes. "Thank you," she said simply and then turned around and walked to the paddle boards. She couldn't help the extra swing in her hips.

She gave them basic instructions and started them on their knees.

"Once you get the feel for it on your knees then you can stand. The first time you do, your legs will be wobbly and it'll take a moment to find your balance. Don't worry if you fall off. That's why we're in shallow water so you can get right back on."

The three beginners balanced on their knees and paddled around the area, staying close to shore. Once they gained confidence each tried to stand up. Megan balanced for a few moments but then fell off. Shelley was standing but when she laughed at her partner that caused her to fall as well.

Brooke stood and immediately looked sure and in control.

"Look at you! Show off," Megan yelled, laughing.

Brooke smiled and her eyes widened as she wobbled just a bit.

Krista was standing in waist deep water when Brooke glided near her. She reached out and gently held the nose of the paddle board. This caused Brooke to almost lose her balance.

Krista looked up at her and said, "You're a natural."

Brooke, obviously pleased with herself, grinned.

Then a devilish look crossed Krista's face. Brooke's eyes widened and she said, "Don't you dare!"

Krista shook the board with her hands and said, "Oops," in an innocent voice.

Brooke was yelling, "Krista!" as she fell off the board and hit the water. When she came up she was laughing.

Krista's face split into the happiest grin. There was that laugh she wanted to hear.

But Brooke was coming after her now and with a leap out of the water she caught Krista on both her shoulders and shoved her under the water.

Krista grabbed Brooke's forearms and yanked her under with her. They both exploded up, laughing and gasping for air.

"That doesn't look like paddle boarding to me!" called Julia from the sand.

Krista swung around, still laughing. "Hey Jules, you should see Brooke, she's a natural."

"I did see until you dumped her. That's what you get!" Julia shouted. "Give it to her again, Brooke!"

Krista looked over at her just as she grabbed her again, dunking her under. She surfaced, laughing. "Okay, okay. Let me breathe!"

Brooke held her shoulders and they both stopped for a moment and stared. Krista saw that flash in Brooke's eyes again and then just as quickly Brooke released her, the connection gone.

"Here," Krista said, reaching for the paddle board. "Get on. I promise I won't dump you again."

Brooke looked at her warily, but crawled on the board. Krista handed her the paddle and steadied the board while Brooke stood up. She gently let go and Brooke paddled away. She watched her and thought about what just happened.

Julia waded out next to Krista. "What was that?"

"I'm not really sure, Jules," Krista said, watching Brooke paddle down the shore. "Yesterday it was like she gradually woke up. When she got to the plane she was closed off and dark. I finally got a bit of a smile out of her. As the day went on she brightened a little more with a full smile or a little laugh. Her face was no longer tight and stern. She loosened up and I think—no, I know she was having a good time. Her entire being was lighter."

"What happened?"

"This morning she came over for coffee and was back to that closed off stoic person. I pushed her a little this morning and found out that she thinks she's helping the women she outs."

"Helping them?"

"Yeah. She said she's helping them live their life openly. And she justified it by saying nothing bad had happened to them after it came out."

"But it's not her place."

"I know," Krista said, shaking her head. "That's what I told her."

"What did she say?"

"I didn't give her a chance," Krista sighed.

"Look at her. Are you sure she hasn't done this before."

"She said she hasn't," Krista said, watching Brooke with a soft smile. Brooke tried to wave at them and almost fell off. Krista giggled and waved back.

Julia had been watching Krista watch Brooke and said, "That's a pretty red swimsuit she's wearing."

"It sure is," Krista said, her voice lowering.

"Krissy," Julia said warily.

"What?"

"Just remember what we're trying to do here."

Krista tore her eyes away from Brooke. "What do you mean? I know exactly what we've got to do."

"You don't see how you're looking at her."

"And just how am I looking at her?"

Julia dropped her head but kept her gaze on Krista. "You're looking at her like you want to tear that pretty red swimsuit off her long, toned body."

"Damn Julia!"

"Well, you are!"

"Sounds like you are."

"Just because I'm married doesn't mean I can't appreciate a beautiful woman. And Brooke Bell is one beautiful, twice-married, questionably principled straight woman."

"I'm not so sure she's as straight as she seems."

"That's not our problem, Krissy. Stopping her from outing our little paradise is, so keep that in mind."

"Oh it's in the front of my mind. You can be sure of that."

11

After lunch Krista rounded up everyone interested in a boat ride and swim at the cliffs. It was an area that had natural bluffs rising out of the water at varied heights. There was easy access from the boat by swimming to the rocks and climbing up to the level your bravery would allow.

Megan, Renee, Shelley, Anna, and Brooke all stepped onto the boat. Becca helped Krista load the food and water. Krista made sure everyone knew where the life jackets were and waited for them to get settled before they left the dock.

"Does anyone need anything?" Krista asked as she started the engine.

A chorus of "All good" answered her.

"Here's sunscreen," she said, passing a bottle to the back of the boat where Anna and Shelley sat. Then she passed another bottle to the front where Megan and Renee had claimed their seats. "Slather it on; you've got to protect your money-maker," she added.

Anna and Shelley laughed. "Not as big a deal for us as you, Krista. We're behind the camera," said Shelley. "Here Brooke, you need it too." She handed Brooke the bottle after she was finished.

"I'm not in front of the camera either," she said, taking the bottle. She rubbed some on her face and then on her arms and legs.

Krista tilted her head and slowly reached her hand over to Brooke's face. "Here," she said, sweeping her thumb under Brooke's bottom lip. "It isn't rubbed in. You should protect your pretty face." She smiled softly and looked up into Brooke's eyes before taking her hand away.

"Thanks," Brooke said faintly.

"Okay. Let's go motorboating," Krista said playfully.

The group gave her a sarcastic groan.

"Hold on," she said, pushing the throttle forward. The front of the boat rose out of the water until they picked up enough speed for it to trim down and then they flew across the lake. It was too noisy at this speed to talk, so everyone leaned back and enjoyed the ride.

After a few minutes Krista reached over and touched Brooke's leg to get her attention. When she looked at her she yelled, "Do you want to drive?"

"What!" Brooke said, her bright blue eyes full of excitement.

"Come on," Krista said, getting up while holding the steering wheel.

Brooke got up. "Is it safe?"

Krista nodded, a big grin on her face as she held the wheel. "Sit down."

Brooke slid into the seat as Krista stood behind.

She leaned down and half-yelled in her ear, "Take the wheel. I'll be right here. You can do it."

Brooke tentatively set her hands on the wheel and when she had a firm grip Krista let go.

The look on Brooke's face did something to Krista's heart. But before she could think about why, Anna yelled, "Way to go, Brooke! Hell yeah!"

The others cheered her on and as Krista started to sit in the now empty seat, Brooke looked over at her, panicked.

"You're fine," Krista said, encouraging her.

Brooke drove them for a few more minutes then Krista got up and switched back with her.

Before Brooke sat down, she leaned into Krista's ear and yelled, "That was so much fun! Thank you!"

Krista grinned and nodded. She slowed the boat down as they approached the cliffs. The reduced speed made it easier to hear one another.

"Does anyone want a drink?" Krista asked her guests.

"Not yet. Maybe after we jump," Anna said.

"This reminds me of that place we shot on location for that spy flick," said Megan.

"Oh yeah, I remember that. The one with Sylvia Stone," Anna said.

"Hey Krista, you dated her, right?" asked Shelley.

"I did," Krista said with her eyes forward as the boat slowly motored closer to the cliffs. She saw Brooke's head turn her way, watching her reaction.

"What happened to you two? It seemed like it got serious and then was over," said Shelley.

"That pretty much explains it."

"Come on, we're all friends here," Renee nudged.

"Well, it turned out she was dating me in an attempt to get on my show."

"No shit!" Shelley barked.

"How did you find out?" asked Anna.

"She told me right after she said she loved me," Krista said with her eyes forward.

"No fucking way!"

"That was my reaction, too. I couldn't believe it. She said she began dating me for the spot on my show and didn't plan on falling in love with me. But she did."

"That's terrible," Brooke said in a low voice.

"Fuck! What happened then? Were you in love with her too?" Megan asked.

"No, but I really liked her. I couldn't believe I'd fallen for it."

"Makes you really wary, doesn't it?" Megan said.

"You haven't dated anyone since, have you?" Shelley asked.

"No. Has that happened to any of you?" Krista asked in an attempt to get the conversation off of her.

"That's kind of how we began," Megan said, leaning over and taking Renee's hand.

"Tell us!" urged Shelley.

"I'd heard about the big queer movie she was directing. I wanted in it so bad I could taste it," Renee said, grinning at Megan. "So, I set out to get in front of her at every opportunity."

Megan laughed. "It was funny. I'd see her at the gym and then there she would be when I was at the coffee shop or doing errands." She looked over at Renee and continued, "But I knew about it from the beginning. I knew she wanted more."

"How did you know?" asked Anna.

"She had every opportunity to shove me in the dressing room and put her tongue down my throat, but she never did. If she was doing it just for the part that's what she'd have done. But instead we went to dinner and dated for awhile before I couldn't stand it any longer and took her home," Megan said, laughing again.

"So, just to be sure, how many times has this dressing room thing happened?" Shelley asked.

Megan laughed. "That hasn't happened to you, Shel? I thought for sure producers were treated that way too."

Shelley threw her head back and laughed. "Not this producer."

Krista cut the engine and threw out the anchor. She unrolled a swim pad and tied it to the boat. "Who wants to go first?"

All eyes were on her then Megan said, "You brought us here. You've got to show us."

"Okay then, follow me," Krista said, jumping into the water.

"I'm going to have a beer first," said Anna.

"There's plenty in the ice chest," Krista yelled from the water.

Krista, Shelley, Megan, and Renee swam over to the rocks. Krista showed them where they could step up and then she climbed up to a cliff that was about ten feet above the water.

"Here goes," she said. "Tawanda!" she screamed as she leaped off the cliff and landed in the water with a splash. She came up and looked back at the divers. "That's all there is to it."

The others took turns jumping and swimming back for another leap. Krista swam over to the swim pad where Brooke was sitting and watching.

"Do you want to jump?"

"I'm not sure yet," she said, watching the others. The air was full of laughter and yelps and screams. "I'm sorry Sylvia Stone did that to you," she said quietly.

Krista looked at her and then shrugged. "Thanks."

"Is that why you haven't dated anyone?"

"Partly, but I also haven't met anyone interesting," she said, staring into Brooke's eyes. "Until recently."

Krista could see Brooke was wrestling with her thoughts and then blurted, "And I'm keeping you from them."

"What?" Krista pulled back, startled. "No you're not."

"If you didn't have to be here with me then you could be with them."

"Why are you concerned about my love life? Besides, the person isn't interested in me."

"How do you know that?"

"I just know. I have a question about yours," Krista said, once again turning the conversation away from her.

"My what?"

"Haven't you been married?"

"Oh. Yes, twice."

"I wanted to get married when I was very young, but it didn't work out. There's never even been anyone I'd consider it with since, except Tara, but that was many years ago."

"I first got married in college. As I look back on it now, it was one of those things where you try to be like everyone else or do what you think you're supposed to do."

"You didn't love him?"

"I did, but more as a friend than a partner. I was young and so messed up."

"What do you mean, messed up?"

"I had a lot of pressure on me to be the golden child. My older brother was the football captain in high school and a successful business major, so I was supposed to follow in his footsteps."

"That's tough."

"Yep. I'd found a love for journalism and wrote for the university paper. He pressured me into dating one of his frat brothers. Anyway, it lasted five years. He kept wanting kids."

"You didn't?"

"No, it wasn't that. I didn't want to bring kids into our unhappiness."

"What happened?"

"That's when I came to LA," she said, looking off in the distance.

"The bright lights, huh," Krista commented.

"Yeah. I tried marriage again and that was a huge disaster," she said firmly.

"Really?"

Brooke eyed Krista warily. "Are you trying to find out my secrets?"

Krista shook her head. "No." She paused. "I can tell you were hurt and I know how that feels."

"Oh come on, Krista. Isn't that part of where we live and the industry? We all get hurt because no one is who they appear to be."

"I can see how you'd think that, but I am exactly what you see. It's too hard to pretend."

"But you did before?"

"No I didn't. I was gay the minute I walked into Hollywood. I never pretended to be straight. Everyone simply assumed I was. The studio arranged dates to be on my arm at award shows, but finally I got through to them to stop that."

"Then why did you come out?"

"The same reason I started this place. If I want to walk down the street and hold a woman's hand I can. That works for me, but it doesn't for everyone. So I started this place for those that want that opportunity, but need discretion."

"Come on, Brooke! You've got to try this!" Shelley yelled.

She smiled and waved at them. "Okay!" Then she turned to Krista. "They've all been so nice to me."

"Of course they have. They're nice people."

"I never doubted they weren't nice people, Krista. I just didn't expect them to be nice to me."

Krista smiled at Brooke. "Come on, let's take a leap."

"What are we leaping into?" Brooke asked cautiously.

"I guess that depends on how far you're willing to go," Krista said, swimming to the cliffs. She had to get away from this woman before she said something she shouldn't. Why did an illicit journalist have to be the first person that actually interested her in years? She splashed the water hard with her hand, relieving some of the frustration coursing through her body.

12

They took turns encouraging one another to leap off higher and higher cliffs. The laughter got louder as the splashes got bigger. Krista kept the music playing, beer and water flowing and even had a few snacks to offer.

"Have you noticed that the more beer Shelley drinks the more outlandish her stories become?" Renee asked playfully.

"I don't know, your stories are quite unbelievable, too," countered Shelley.

"Oh I didn't say yours were unbelievable. I believe every word! You're just getting better and better at telling them."

Anna and Brooke laughed along with Krista. They were all lying half on and half off the swimming pad, enjoying the cool water and the hot sun.

Megan swam up and hoisted herself right in the middle of everyone. She fell on her back and said, "Brooke, if you decide to write an article about this hideaway, please don't give out the location. This has been the perfect day."

"It has," said Anna. "Why aren't there more people around?"

"It gets busy on weekends, but during the week it's usually just the locals. That's why we offer the trips for the entire week. You'll notice more people on the lake beginning Friday afternoon."

"This is so nice," Brooke said, trailing her hand through the water.

"Don't get too comfortable, it's about time for us to start back. Anyone want to take one more jump?"

"I have an idea," Megan said, sitting up. "Let's all jump off together holding hands."

"Aw, isn't she the cutest," Renee said, sliding into the water. "Come on, babe. I'm game."

Anna looked at Shelley, "What do you say, honey? Want to take a leap with me?" She wiggled her eyebrows and Shelley giggled. They both slid off the pad and started toward the cliffs.

Anna stopped and looked back. "Hey, aren't you coming?"

"Come on, Brooke. Come on Krista!" Megan yelled, standing on the first cliff.

Krista turned to Brooke. "You don't have to do this if you don't want to."

A smile spread across Brooke's lips until her whole face lit up. "Will you hold my hand?" she said, her words dripping with sarcasm.

Krista chuckled. "I sure will."

They swam to the cliffs and joined the others. There wasn't enough room for all six of them to jump at the same time so they went in pairs.

Megan and Renee went first, screaming and laughing until they hit the water. When she came up Megan said, "Wait! Don't jump!" She quickly swam to the boat and climbed in.

"Let me get your picture when you jump," she said, holding up her phone.

Anna and Shelley were next. Anna counted them down. "Three, two, one!" she shouted. They jumped out, kicked up their feet and hit the water still holding hands.

"I got it!" Megan yelled. "That was great! Okay Brooke and Krista, it's your turn."

Brooke turned to Krista and held out her hand. "Hold on tight."

Krista grinned. "You know I will." She took Brooke's hand, intertwining their fingers, and squeezed.

"Do I?" Brooke asked.

"One," Krista started counting.

"Two," Brooke said with her.

"Three!" they said together and leaped.

Megan looked at the picture as they swam back to the boat. She showed it to Renee and said, "Look at this."

Megan had captured Krista's face full of wonder and delight, staring at Brooke. She stared back at Krista with an amazed look of joy.

"If you didn't know them, you'd think they're crazy in love from this picture," Renee said. "Wow."

"That's what I thought," said Megan.

"What's the matter?" asked Anna.

"Nothing," Megan said. "I'll text the pic to you when we get back."

"Time to go, cliff divers," Krista said, getting back into the boat.

When everyone was settled with drinks and snacks, Krista rolled the swim pad up with Brooke's help and secured it.

"I think we have to keep this perfect day going," said Shelley.

"Me too!" Renee said.

"Let's change and hit the bar when we get back. It's time for some dancing," said Anna, standing up, twirling around, and sitting back down.

"Let's go," Krista said, putting the boat in gear. She sneaked a look over at Brooke and was surprised to find her smiling right back at her.

"Do you want to drive again?"

Brooke shook her head and wrinkled her nose. "I'll just watch you."

"Okay," Krista said slowly. Their eyes were locked on one another's before Krista finally had to tear hers away to drive the boat.

Courtney and Becca met them at the dock and helped everyone get out of the boat.

"We'll clean everything up, Aunt Krissy," Courtney said.

"Thanks," Krista said.

"Well, you do pay us," added Becca.

Krista chuckled. "Yes, but it's nice not to have to ask you to do your job."

"Okay, let's meet at the bar in an hour," announced Anna.

Everyone agreed and made their way up the walkway. Brooke was waiting for Krista in the driver's side of the golf cart.

"Hop in," she said, grinning.

Krista smirked and sat beside her. "Am I safe?"

Brooke tilted her head. "About as safe as I am with you."

Krista laughed and pointed forward with one hand. "Lead on!"

Brooke pushed the accelerator and off they went.

"Hey Krissy," she teased

Krista chuckled. "Yes B?"

"Do you ever take boat rides at night?"

"We could go see the sun set. There would be enough light left for us to get back before it's too dark. I don't really like to drive on the lake at night."

"Could we do that tomorrow?"

Krista looked over at her. "Sure." She paused. "That would be nice."

Brooke pulled up to her cabin and they both got out.

"I'll walk from here," Krista said. "I'm going to take a quick shower. Come on over when you're ready." Krista walked a few steps then stopped. She turned back to Brooke. "Hey, did you have a good time today?"

"You couldn't tell?"

"Just making sure. You didn't feel uncomfortable, did you?"

Brooke's brow furrowed. "Not at all. Why do you ask?"

"You'd tell me if you were, right?"

"Yes," Brooke said. "What are you getting at?"

Krista sighed. "You're a straight woman hanging with a bunch of lesbians that have been drinking. I simply don't want you to feel uncomfortable, especially since we're going to the bar with more drinking and adding dancing to that."

Brooke smiled kindly at Krista. "Thanks for looking out for me, Aunt Krissy."

"Brooke," Krista said, dipping her head.

"It's fine, Krista. I promise to tell you if I'm uncomfortable. Okay?"

"Okay." Krista turned around and walked to her cabin, not sure why she'd asked that question. Despite this morning's rough start, Brooke felt more like a friend than a guest today. This afternoon reminded her more of a girls' trip than an outing from a resort.

She took a quick shower and got dressed. As she drank from a cold bottle of water she heard Brooke step onto the back porch.

"Come in," she called from the kitchen through the screen door.

Brooke walked in and saw the bottle of water. "That's probably a good idea."

Krista handed her one. "You've got to pace yourself. I've learned that women on vacation love to party."

Brooke chuckled. "How about you? Do you love to party?"

"I just want everyone to have a good time."

"Do you think you could stop worrying about me having a good time and just enjoy yourself tonight?"

Krista laughed. "I have been having a good time."

"Really?"

Krista nodded. "Except," she narrowed her eyes and looked at Brooke, "this morning was a little confusing."

Brooke looked away. "I know."

"Everything is all right now? Right?"

Brooke met Krista's gaze and nodded.

Krista smiled. "Well, let's go to the bar."

Brooke's face brightened. "Let's go."

They walked into the bar and found Allison and Libby having a drink.

Krista walked over and stood between them with her arms around each woman's shoulders. "You are about to be overrun by a group of tipsy lesbians having a dance party."

"We haven't been dancing in ages," Allison said, grinning. "Wanna dance, babe?" she said, looking over at Libby.

"Heck yeah!" Libby said, getting up and offering Allison her hand. Music was already playing and Krista turned it up a little louder.

"I'm going to push these tables together so we can all be together," Krista said, walking to the edge of the dance floor.

"I'll help," Brooke said from one end of the table.

"You're not trying to get a job here, are you? First you help on the boat and now here," Krista teased.

"It does look like a lot of fun."

"You might want to ask Courtney and Becca about that."

"Are we having a party?" Julia asked, walking up to them.

"We are. Why don't you call Heidi and see if she wants to come out? I'm going to tell Chef to make several platters of appetizers. I need to get food in this crowd."

"I'll tell her when I call Heidi."

Krista looked over at Brooke. She was staring at Allison and Libby. "Is that upsetting to you, Brooke?" Krista asked, standing beside her.

"Not at all," she said softly. "I can't take my eyes off of them. They look at one another with such love."

Krista smiled, nodding, "And they've been together twenty years! Can you imagine that?"

The cliff divers came in and the noise level instantly rose.

"Want to help me choose songs on the jukebox?" Krista asked Brooke.

"Sure. I can't believe you have a jukebox."

"It just looks like one. It has hundreds of songs and we can create our own playlists."

They took turns making selections and then walked back over to the table. Julia walked up with a pitcher of pink punch and set it on the table.

"Is that your Lesbian Licker?" Brooke asked.

Krista's eyebrows shot up her forehead and then she burst out laughing. Brooke looked mortified when she realized what she'd said and then she started laughing too.

"That's a better name for our signature drink." Krista continued to giggle.

Julia poured and handed each of them a glass. "My wonderful wife will be here soon."

"Oh good. Looks like we're having a party!"

"Does the entire group usually get together like this?" asked Brooke, watching the couples on the dance floor.

"Not always, but it's happened a few times," Julia said.

"Are you going to dance with me?" Krista asked, capturing Brooke's gaze with her own.

"Oh Krista, I haven't danced in a hundred years," she said, her eyes wide.

"I haven't either. We'll be perfect together."

"Okay." Brooke smiled shyly. "But let me finish this drink. I think I'll need it."

"Hey, you two, come on!" Shelley yelled from the dance floor.

"On our way," Krista said, putting her off.

Brooke had a relieved look on her face as she sipped her drink. She leaned over and said to Krista, "I was thinking about what you said earlier about being uncomfortable." Krista nodded. "Do you think sometimes being uncomfortable could be a good thing?"

"Mmm, I guess it could be. Why?"

"I don't know, this whole week is definitely out of my comfort zone. But I'm having such a good time and it's only the second day."

Krista smiled. "You know what, Brooke? It means a lot to me for you to have a good time, no matter what happens when you go back to LA. In just two days I've learned that you don't get to be yourself and you don't ever relax."

"Why do you say that?" Brooke looked at her warily.

"Because you're having a good time! I can tell you don't do that often. This Brooke that's here with me is a person I'd like to get to know, a person I'd want for a friend."

Brooke sat back, obviously stunned.

Oh no, Krista thought. *I've done it now.* "I'm sorry. I've upset you."

"Do you mean that?" Booke asked, intensely staring into Krista's eyes.

"Yes! I told you I'd be honest with you."

Brooke shook her head, but her eyes kept staring. "No one wants to be my friend," she said quietly.

Krista decided to take a chance. She reached for Brooke's hand and grasped it. Then she nodded toward the women laughing on the dance floor. "Those women out there would want to be your friend, too."

Brooke looked at her, unbelieving.

"Come on, let's dance and see just how much more uncomfortable you can be." Krista stood, still holding Brooke's hand. She didn't resist, so Krista led them to the dance floor.

13

Brooke tugged on Krista's hand. When she turned toward her Brooke said, "I don't want to embarrass you."

"What?" Krista said with a kind smile. "You can't embarrass me or yourself for that matter. We're dancing," she said, walking them onto the dance floor. She held her hand and started to move a little. "There's no good or bad in dancing. Everyone is perfect."

Brooke gave her a tentative smile and began to move. Krista dropped her hand and raised her arms above her head and began to swing her hips with the music. Brooke found her rhythm and as the song continued her smile grew.

They danced for another song and Brooke's smile never left her face.

"Who chose this song?" Anna yelled. "It's my favorite!"

Brooke shot her hand up and waved. "I did!" she yelled, twirling around.

When that song was over they went back to the table for a drink. Heidi had arrived and she and Julia were dancing to a slow song. Krista noticed once again Brooke was staring.

"They fit together," she said, leaning over so Krista could hear her.

"It wasn't always that way, believe me," Krista said, smiling at the dancing couple.

"Really?"

"Yeah, they didn't see eye to eye on some things and were both a tad stubborn at first. But when they realized there were so many more things they did agree on and that they could work through the ones they disagreed on and, well…" Krista said, chuckling.

"What? Well what?"

"Then Heidi kissed her and it was all over." She laughed.

Brooke looked at her, confused. "What do you mean? One kiss and that was it?"

"They were in the middle of a disagreement and Heidi was so exasperated with Julia because she kept interrupting her, so she shut her up with a kiss. You should've seen Jules' face! It was priceless."

"You were there?"

"Oh yeah, I can't remember what they were discussing but when Heidi kissed Julia she didn't say another word. She grabbed Heidi's hand and they left."

"Whoa!" Brooke said, amazed. She stared at them as they came to the table.

"What's the matter?" asked Julia with a grin.

"I just told her about the kiss," Krista said, shrugging.

"Oh." Julia nodded.

"Is she telling me the truth?"

"Well, Krissy doesn't lie, most of the time," Julia teased.

"What?" Krista said, leaning back, stunned.

"I'm kidding," Julia said, throwing an arm around her shoulders. "Yep. This one was tired of my big mouth and gave me a kiss that shut me the fuck up. Right, darlin'?"

Krista burst out laughing. "I didn't explain it quite like that."

"She wasn't tired of my mouth later. I'll tell you that for sure," Julia said, leaning in and winking.

"Oh shit. You did not just say that."

Julia threw her head back and laughed. "I sure did."

"Oh no, excuse me while I go to the restroom," Krista said, getting up.

Brooke's eyes widened.

"You'll be okay," Krista chuckled, winked at her and walked off.

While she was washing her hands in the restroom, Megan walked in. "Hey, I texted you the picture of you and Brooke from the cliffs."

"Oh, thanks. I'll check my phone," Krista said, drying her hands.

"Zoom in on your faces. It's a really good picture."

Krista wrinkled her brow. "Okay..."

"You'll see. She's into you."

"What?"

"Renee and I can tell. You should see the two of you on the dance floor."

"We're just having fun, Meg."

"I'm just making an observation. Do you think the more fun she has the less likely she is to write the article?"

"That's not why she's here. I mean, I want her to have a good time, but I want her to see why this place is special. I want her to see that she can be herself."

"I think you're bringing out the best in her. She's fun to be around and I never imagined that," Megan said, walking into a stall.

Krista nodded and looked at herself in the mirror. She had a sparkle in her eyes that hadn't been there in a long time. *Hmm.* "See ya, Megan." she said, leaving the restroom.

When she got back to the table Julia was entertaining Brooke with stories from their summers working here.

"You let the air out of a guy's tires?" Brooke asked, amused.

Krista gave Julia an admonishing look. "It was just one tire. He deserved it; he was an asshole."

"Do you want to dance again?" Brooke asked.

"Yes!" Krista said, jumping up. "Anything to get you away from Jules and her Krissy stories."

On the way to the dance floor Brooke said, "I was enjoying her stories and learning about you."

"Just ask. I'll tell you anything you want to know."

"It sounds like you were a lot of fun," Brooke said, swinging her arms.

"I still am!" Krista yelled over the music.

They both laughed and moved to the music. When that song ended a slow song began. Krista looked at Brooke and raised her eyebrows. Surprisingly, Brooke stayed where she was.

Krista opened her arms and Brooke took a step toward her.

"I don't want to make you uncomfortable," Krista said.

Brooke put her arms around Krista's shoulders and Krista put her hands on Brooke's hips as the sounds of "Runaway" by Jefferson Starship filtered around the bar.

"I like this song," she said into Brooke's ear. Krista pulled her a little closer so she could run one hand up and down her back. "Relax," she said. "It's me. We jump off cliffs together, remember? " Krista's eyes sparkled as she pulled her head back to look into Brooke's eyes.

Brooke's eyes were a dark blue and she replied, "I can trust you, right?"

Krista stared into those dazzling blue eyes. "That's right. You can trust me, Brooke." Krista felt the tension leave Brooke's body and she smiled, pulling her a little closer.

They swayed to the music and Krista simply enjoyed holding a woman close again. A beautiful woman at that.

When the song was finished she stepped back and said, "Thank you, Brooke."

Brooke nodded and they walked back to the table.

The party began to wind down as Allison and Libby waved goodbye to everyone.

"Do you have to stay until everyone leaves?" Brooke asked Krista.

"Are you ready to go? I can take you to the cabin."

"No, I just wondered."

Krista looked around and turned back to Brooke. "We can go. I think everyone else is ready to leave."

Julia overheard her and said, "Go ahead. We're having the last dance and we'll make sure everyone gets to their cabins safely."

"Okay." Krista kissed Heidi on the cheek and hugged Julia. "See you tomorrow."

"Thanks for a wonderful evening, Julia," Brooke said.

"Anytime," Julia replied with a smile.

"It was nice to see you, Heidi."

"Nice to see you, Brooke. Enjoy the rest of your night," Heidi said.

They left the bar and got into the golf cart. "Would you like to sit by the water for a while? It's still relatively early."

"That sounds really nice. Isn't this cool breeze lovely?" said Brooke.

"It is," Krista replied.

She drove them to their cabins and Brooke hopped out. "I'm going to run in and get a bottle of water. Would you like one?"

"Yes, please."

When Brooke came back out they walked down to the water and sat in the chairs. Neither said anything for a few minutes while they drank their water and enjoyed the night.

"This has been such a good day. I can't remember when I had this much fun," Brooke said, looking out over the water.

"Same for me," Krista said, taking another drink.

"Really? I thought you did this all the time here."

"No, I don't. I take groups to the cliffs and show them how to paddle board, but I don't enjoy it like I did today. It felt more like I was on vacation *with* you." Krista chuckled.

"I haven't danced like that since college, I guess."

"I occasionally dance with Julia and Heidi or one of the girls."

They could hear the water lapping on the sand just in front of their feet.

"Brooke, I'm having a hard time equating the woman that writes those articles with the woman I spent the day with."

"Because?" Brooke said, glancing Krista's way.

"The tone of those articles makes it seem like you don't like gay women, but today we were all friends." When Brooke didn't say anything Krista asked, "Do you not like me?"

"What?" Brooke said, whipping her head around. "I do like you, Krista. I'm just getting to know you, but I've always liked you."

"You've always liked me?" Krista said, tilting her head, puzzled.

"What I mean is that I know we don't run in the same circles, but you've always been a celebrity that I knew was a good person."

"Then why did you want to write an article about me being gay before I came out?"

Brooke sighed and put her face in her hands.

"Talk to me, Brooke. I know something happened to you."

Brooke looked over at her. "How do you know?"

"Something had to happen to make you not like gay women. I just know."

Brooke slowly nodded. "You said I could trust you."

"You can."

"I don't hate gay women, Krista." She exhaled loudly and ran her fingers through her hair. "I don't know how to start."

Her blonde locks shone in the moonlight and Krista's heart ached for the struggle she witnessed on her face. "One of those girls was you, wasn't it?"

"What?" she whispered, looking over at Krista.

"The two girls you told me about in your high school. One of them was you."

Brooke slowly nodded. Krista could see the tears in her eyes and it broke her heart. She got up and kneeled next to her and took her hand. "It's okay. Tell me what happened."

Brooke's glassy eyes met hers and she squeezed her hand. "We were so careful, but my brother caught us kissing one night in my room."

"Oh Brooke," Krista whispered.

"He told me if I didn't end it with her he'd tell the whole school. Then he spread rumors about her and no one wanted to be her friend after that. I couldn't be around her anymore or everyone would know I was the girl that had been with her." Her voice broke and tears rolled down her cheeks.

Krista waited patiently for her to continue.

"I shunned her just like the rest of the girls did." She wiped the tears with her hands. "I can still see the hurt in her eyes when they called her names. She looked at me," Brooke said, sobbing hard. "She was so hurt and I walked away laughing with the rest of them so they wouldn't suspect." Brooke broke down, leaned over, and Krista took her in her arms. She held her while she sobbed. Krista stroked her hair and spoke softly, telling her everything would be all right.

"I can't believe I'm telling you all this. I barely know you." Brooke sniffled between sobs.

"Sometimes it's easier to tell someone you don't know. You don't have to worry about what they think."

Brooke pulled back so she could see Krista's eyes. "But I care what you think."

Krista gave her a compassionate smile. "You were a kid, Brooke. A kid that was bullied into being someone else."

"You don't think I'm a horrible person?"

"No! You were a victim, too. I'm so sorry you had to go through this." Krista stroked her back, trying to ease some of the tension she could feel in Brooke's body.

"But I loved her, Krista. How could I hurt someone I loved like that?"

"It's usually the ones we hurt the most because we do love them."

"And I don't want you to think I didn't love my husband because I did. We just wanted different things."

"I'm sure you did love him. I believe you." Krista could feel Brooke soften and then she heard her stifle a yawn.

Krista released her and stood up. "I can see you're tired. Why don't I put you to bed?"

"All of sudden I am drained."

"Holding in guilt is hard, Brooke. Letting it go can be even harder. You know they say salt water is healing."

Brooke looked up at her and shook her head. "I'm not understanding."

"Tears are salt water. Crying is healing. Let it go, B," Krista said softly.

Brooke continued to look at her as she processed Krista's words. A small smile crossed her face when Krista offered her hand.

"Come on." She smiled down at her.

They walked into the cabin and Krista led her to the bedroom. "Why don't you change and get into bed. I'll get you some water."

Krista walked out and got her a glass of water and waited a few minutes before going back to the bedroom. Brooke was in bed under the covers, so she set the glass on the bedside table and sat on the edge of the bed.

Before Krista could say anything Brooke said, "That's not why I wrote the articles, Krista, but that's how it started." She blinked. "What are we doing tomorrow?"

"I thought it would be fun to ride bikes. You can ride a bike, can't you?"

"Yes."

"There's a nice trail that begins inside the property then runs down to a little private beach. We can pack a lunch and swim. Or it would be a great place to talk."

Brooked nodded. "I'd like to tell you the rest. I don't know why," she said with tears stinging her eyes, "but I want to tell you everything. I don't want you to hate me."

Krista scoffed. "I don't hate you."

"Not yet," she said softly.

Krista shook her head. "I'm going to sit right over here," she said, indicating the chair in the corner of the room, "until you fall asleep. Then in the morning I'll text you when the coffee is ready. I want you to come to my cabin with a smile on your face, not the scowl that greeted me this morning."

Brooke gave her a small smile. "I'll try."

"No trying. Do it, Brooke," Krista said firmly.

Brooke nodded.

Krista got up and turned the bedside table lamp off. The light from the living room shone through the doorway, but otherwise it was dark.

"Thanks, Krista," Brooke said quietly and rolled over.

Krista sat down and watched Brooke's back rise and fall in the moonlight. Her theory about Brooke's high school years proved correct. She wondered what happened after that. All she knew was that Brooke was hurt and that pain led her to those dreadful articles. Krista felt a sadness envelop her along with the darkness. How many kids had this happened to? It was probably still happening. Some of these kids reacted like Brooke and hurt others because they were hurt. When would the cycle be broken?

14

Krista sat on the porch with her cup of coffee. She breathed in the sweet morning air and waited on Brooke. It wasn't long until she heard Brooke's screen door close and she watched her walk over. She stepped up on the porch with a hint of a smile, but she looked Krista in the eyes, unlike yesterday morning.

Krista got up and put both hands on Brooke's shoulders. "Good morning." She took her right hand and put it over Brooke's heart. She could see the surprise in Brooke's eyes but she didn't look away. "Is your heart beating fast?" Krista asked, knowing Brooke felt awkward about last night.

"Yes, I..." Brooke said, a smile beginning at the corners of her mouth.

"We're going to have a wonderful day," Krista said, putting her hand back on Brooke's shoulder. "Okay?"

"Okay." Brooke nodded and let the smile reach her eyes.

Krista caught herself staring at those bright blue eyes for a moment too long. "Would you like coffee?" she asked, dropping her arms.

"Yes." Brooke nodded.

"You know where it is," Krista said, pointing with her thumb to the back door.

Brooke went inside and Krista sat back down and sipped her coffee. A part of her wished she and Brooke could forget about the reasons they were here and enjoy getting to know one another. She knew Brooke needed to tell the rest of her story and Krista wanted to hear it. Maybe tomorrow they could put all of this behind them for the day and just enjoy one another. Was that a crazy idea?

She hadn't been able to go right to sleep last night. Thoughts of Brooke's sadness and the pain that dulled those blue eyes she'd become so fond of gazing into kept flashing through her mind. Of course she wanted to ease that pain for her. What person wouldn't? But Krista knew there was more going on inside her than helping a person in pain. There was something pulling her to Brooke Bell. She couldn't keep from wondering if Brooke felt it too.

Her screen door quietly closed and Brooke sat in the chair next to her.

"Did you sleep well?" Krista asked, looking out over the lake. It was such a beautiful morning; a light breeze rippled through the leaves sounding almost like a lullaby. *It'd be nice to sit here all morning*, Krista thought.

"I don't think I moved all night. I heard birds singing out my window and couldn't believe it was already morning. How about you?" Brooke looked over at Krista.

"Oh? Uh, I slept okay," Krista said, not expecting the question.

Brooke's brow furrowed. "You sure?"

Krista sighed and glanced over at Brooke and then back to the water. "Yes. It's just so nice this morning. I love it when there's a hint of a breeze like this. It makes me want to sit here all morning."

"Why can't we?"

Krista raised a brow. "I guess we could." Then her stomach growled loudly. She looked down and then over to Brooke and they both laughed.

"Maybe not all morning," Brooke said.

Krista sighed. "You know, Brooke, I want to ask you for a favor."

"Okay. What do you need?"

"I know we have things to talk about today, but I don't want it to loom over us. Let's plan to talk at the beach when we have our picnic. That way we both can enjoy the bike ride and each other."

"That sounds nice because it's already been weighing on me."

"I'm sure it has. Here's the favor."

"Oh, okay. I thought that was it."

Krista looked her in the eyes. "Do you think tomorrow we could forget about the article, the resort, and why we're here…and just be on vacation together?"

Brooke tilted her head. "Is that realistic, though? Would you really be on vacation with me?"

"After getting to know you, yes. I certainly would."

A smile grew on Brooke's face. "That would be amazing, Krista. I'd love it."

"Good. We're still going to have a wonderful day today, but tomorrow is something to look forward to," Krista said, smiling back at Brooke. They held one another's gaze and Krista asked softly, "What?"

"Your eyes," Brooke said. "They're the most beautiful shade of blue. So clear and kind."

Krista grinned. "How funny because I think the same about yours. I think they're darker than mine and so beautiful."

Brooke looked down shyly and then back up at Krista. Neither of them said anything as they continued to stare. Then it was Brooke's stomach's turn to get noisy, ending the moment.

Krista's eyes widened. "Let's get breakfast!"

She took Brooke's cup and set them both inside. They got into the golf cart and went to the restaurant.

After they'd placed their orders Krista turned to Brooke. "I need to talk to Julia for a few minutes about the day's activities. After we eat we can go to the kitchen and see what we can find for our picnic."

"It's okay, Krista," Brooke said, chuckling. "I can sit by myself for a few minutes."

"We'll keep you company," Libby said as she and Allison walked in.

"Good morning," Krista greeted them. "We'd love for you to join us. I'll be right back." Krista said, leaving to find Julia.

"Hey," Krista said, walking into the kitchen. "Heidi didn't have a headache this morning, did she?"

Julia chuckled. "No, but she didn't want to get up." Julia winked at Krista. "We had a lot of fun last night."

It was Krista's turn to chuckle, but she also felt a pang of envy. She'd been single for so long and sometimes she missed having someone to share good times with.

"You okay?" Julia asked, putting an arm around her.

"Yeah. Can you handle everything today? Brooke and I are going to ride bikes to the beach and have a picnic. I'm not sure about later this afternoon."

"How's that going? Has she opened up to you?"

"She did last night. Her brother of all people almost outed her in high school."

"So she is gay?"

"No, I think bisexual. She's been carrying around so much guilt because he outed her girlfriend, and then Brooke turned her back on her to save herself."

"Fuck! Why can't they just leave us alone!"

"I know, Jules. Anyway, she has more to tell me, so we're going to talk at the beach. She said the oddest thing."

"What's that?"

"That she's afraid I'm going to hate her." She turned to Julia. " I couldn't hate her. Especially knowing what happened to her in high school."

"We were lucky in high school, weren't we?" Julia commented.

"Yeah, thank goodness we had each other. Who knows what would have happened if we'd actually had girlfriends."

"She's a very beautiful woman, Krissy. And you two looked like you were having a really good time last night." Julia had a hint of warning in her voice.

"What are you not saying, Julia?" Krista asked defensively.

"Uh-oh."

"What?"

"Remember you're trying to save our place."

"I'm well aware of what we're trying to do, Julia."

"Easy now. You didn't see how Brooke was looking at you last night. I'm just saying, be careful."

Krista sighed and looked at her best friend. "There's something about her, Jules. I like her. How in the hell did that happen?" She blew out a breath.

Julia smiled. "I know you do."

"You do?"

"Yeah. I could tell the minute you got off the plane."

"What!"

"I know you, Krissy. It'll be okay."

"I hope so."

"Go have fun today. There's nothing wrong with having a good time with a beautiful woman. I did last night," she said, wiggling her eyebrows.

Krista chuckled. "And you just happened to marry her."

"No happening about it. I knew she was the one for me."

"I'll find my Heidi someday. Now, I'd better get back out there."

Krista left and Julia shook her head. "I think you may have, my dear friend. You just don't know it yet."

Brooke and Allison were laughing at an animated Libby when Krista joined them.

"I hear you're going bike riding today," Allison said.

"We are." Krista hesitated and glanced at Brooke. "Would you like to come along?" she asked, feeling obligated to offer.

"No thanks," said Allison with a knowing smile. "Maybe another time."

Krista wondered if she'd missed something, but their food came and they all dug in. After breakfast they went to the kitchen to prepare their picnic and Krista drove them back to the cabin to change and then to the bikes.

"I have to admit I'm excited about this," Brooke said, adjusting her backpack. "It's been a long time since I've ridden a bike on a trail. We rode everywhere when we were kids."

"I know what you mean. I've been riding these trails for years."

"Even after you left?"

"Yeah, sometimes when I'd come back we'd take the girls to ride bikes or Julia and I would."

Brooke looked over at her. "It must be wonderful to have a friend that's known you for years."

Krista chuckled. "Most of the time." She turned her bike toward the trails. "You ready?"

Brooke got on her bike and started pedaling.

The trail was dappled with sunlight. It was fairly easy going with a few rolling hills. They didn't talk much because they couldn't ride side by side. Krista stopped a couple of times to warn Brooke of particularly challenging parts of the trail.

Brooke rolled up beside Krista, who was straddling her bike. She motioned for her to be quiet.

"Look right through there," Krista whispered.

Brooke leaned over and followed Krista's pointing finger to where two deer stood with their heads down, eating. Her face lit up and she stifled a gasp.

Krista looked over at Brooke's delight and their helmets nearly bonked together they were so close. Her heart skipped a beat when Brooke slowly turned toward her. She looked down at her lips and then back up into Brooke's eyes. Krista could feel and hear her heart pounding in her ears.

About that time the deer looked up and saw them, scampering away and rustling the brush. They both looked back at the deer and could just see them disappear in the trees.

Krista saw Brooke swallow and turn back to her. Her gaze was locked on Krista's eyes and then she looked down at her lips and began to lean in. Krista's eyes began to close and anticipation hung in the air between them. Then their helmets banged together before their lips met. Krista's eyes flew open as her head rebounded back and she saw Brooke was just as surprised.

They laughed softly and leaned back.

Brooke shook her head, a red tint spreading over her cheeks. "I've got moves, Krissy. You'd better watch out."

Krista dropped her head and giggled as Brooke threw her leg over her bike. "Come on, it's not much further to the beach."

The trail opened up to a small clearing with a beautiful view of the lake. Just as Krista promised there was a small sandy beach waiting for them and their picnic.

"This is beautiful," Brooke said, leaning her bike against a tree and taking her backpack off.

"Isn't it?" Krista set her backpack down and took a large towel out, spreading it onto the ground.

"How about a swim before we eat?" asked Krista, already taking her shorts and shirt off.

Brooke wasn't shy about watching Krista undress. She was wearing a cobalt blue two piece suit that fit her perfectly. "Wow, that's a beautiful color on you," she said.

"This old thing?" Krista said, using her best Southern drawl. "You know, I decided this year when I turned fifty I was wearing what I wanted. This is one of my favorite suits. I don't have the body I did when I was younger, but I really don't care."

"You look even better," Brooke said breathlessly.

Krista smiled at her and walked toward the water swinging her hips. "Come on!"

Brooke quickly undressed and joined her. They swam out a little ways and floated on their backs, letting the water rinse the trail dust from their bodies.

"This is so nice," Brooke said.

"Mmm," Krista moaned. She peeked over at Brooke and watched her float serenely. Then an evil grin grew on her face as she leaped up and pushed her under the water. Brooke came up flailing and gasping for breath.

Krista laughed. "Pay back for yesterday."

"Oh you," Brooke said, reaching for Krista.

Krista started backing up, but then her foot slipped on the sandy bottom and Brooke grabbed her. Krista threw her arms around Brooke's neck and held on.

"You're going under with me," she said, hugging Brooke close.

Brooke laughed and supported them both in the chest deep water. "Okay, okay. I won't dunk you again."

Krista eased her grip and pulled back so they were face to face. She watched the droplets of water run down Brooke's cheeks and then over her lips. "Want to try those moves again, B?" she asked breathlessly.

Brooke leaned in and pressed her lips to Krista's. The softness of Brooke's lips coupled with the firmness of the kiss made Krista weak in the knees even though they were in water. A small moan escaped her throat and she tightened her arms around Brooke's neck.

Those soft lips fit perfectly against hers and when she felt them part slightly, Krista ran her tongue along Brooke's bottom lip then gently pushed past her lips. When her tongue met Brooke's she lost her breath and felt Brooke's arms tighten around her.

This might be the best first kiss Krista had ever had. She heard Brooke moan as their tongues continued a dance of exploration. They finally eased apart and Krista quickly kissed Brooke's lips again.

"You do have moves," Krista said, her arms still around Brooke's neck.

Brooke looked away and chuckled. "Please. I know better."

Krista captured her eyes and then her lips followed. This kiss started soft, but quickly escalated as Krista ran her hand through Brooke's golden hair. Their tongues were silky and sensual as they searched for pleasure in one another.

They pulled apart, both panting. Brooke held Krista in her arms and Krista cupped Brooke's face and grinned. She tilted her head. "Maybe we'd better have that picnic now."

Brooke returned her smile and nodded. She released Krista, but took her hand as they walked out of the water together.

At this moment Krista didn't care about the rest of Brooke's story or that this was her resort. All she cared about was that kiss and doing it again.

They sat down on the towel and before Krista began to get the food out she stopped and turned to Brooke.

"You know, in this place, it's like the world falls away," Krista said, leaning back on her hands. "It's just you and me," she added, looking intensely in Brooke's eyes. The smile that Brooke gave her went right to her core.

Brooke leaned down and gently pushed Krista all the way onto her back. She hovered over her briefly and then cupped the side of her face. The look she gave Krista was full of emotion and her eyes were midnight blue. She softly placed her lips on Krista's and then claimed her mouth, caressing, nipping, and nibbling. Krista's arms were around Brooke's neck again, pulling her closer. It was as if they'd done this all their lives.

When they both needed to take a breath, Brooke pulled back slightly as Krista ran her hand through Brooke's hair. "I could kiss you all day long," Brooke whispered.

"Mmm," Krista moaned. "I'd like that."

15

Brooke stared into Krista's eyes, searching.

"What are you looking for?" Krista whispered.

"Doubt? I can't believe I'm kissing you."

"I want this," Krista said, pulling Brooke back down and kissing away any doubt.

When they came up for air, Brooke said, "I have to ask. How many women have you brought here?"

Krista chuckled. "Just you."

"Not even Tara?"

Krista furrowed her brow. "Not even Tara. Why would you ask about her?"

"She's just made it known that someday you'll be together again."

"Seriously? That has to be another rumor," Krista said, stroking Brooke's hair. "It's not happening. That was a long time ago. We're friends, that's all." She smiled at Brooke. "I don't need to worry about anyone coming after me, do I?"

Brooke leaned down and kissed Krista softly. "Do you know how long it's been since I've kissed a woman?"

"Do you know how long it's been since *I've* kissed a woman?"

Brooke smiled. "There's no one, Krissy. And there hasn't been for a long time."

Krista could see the sadness in Brooke's eyes. "Is that a sacrifice that came along with the articles?"

"Kind of."

Krista took Brooke's face into her hands. "I know you need to tell me what happened and I want to hear it, but I want this to continue." She kissed Brooke softly. "Do you want this to continue?"

"More than anything," Brooke breathed.

Krista's heart drummed in her chest. What she really wanted right now was to be naked with this woman with no other care in the world but to make her come over and over again. She wanted to taste her, she wanted to be inside her, she wanted to kiss every inch of her body. This sudden passion she realized had been building since the day Brooke strutted toward her in that diner.

"You seem to have a way of making me forget things because all I want to do is this," she said, pulling Brooke back down and ravishing her lips.

Brooke moaned and Krista felt her body press down into hers. They were skin to skin where their suits didn't cover and she could feel the warmth. She could also feel the heat building inside her and was pretty sure Brooke felt it too.

When they broke apart panting, Krista asked, "Why have you sacrificed your own happiness, Brooke? I can see you like being with me."

"Like? My God, Krista! Like doesn't begin to cover what you do to me," Brooke said, her eyes wide and dark with desire. "But you've sacrificed too. Why?"

Krista ran her thumb over Brooke's bottom lip and her cheek. Then she started to get up and Brooke eased off her. She took Brooke's hand in her own as they sat knee to knee.

"There hasn't been another woman that I've wanted to kiss and touch the way I do you in a very long time, so I'll try not to smother you."

Brooke smiled. "You won't smother me."

Krista looked into her eyes. "It took me a long time to move on from Tara. I understood why she left me, but that didn't change how much it hurt. She was my everything. We were best friends and did everything together, including career moves. I was devastated. I didn't date anyone for over a year and then after that I had a girlfriend or two, but nothing lasted more than a couple of years. I'd made up my mind that I wasn't going to be hurt like that ever again. Then after I came out, there was the mess with Sylvia that I told you about."

"She wanted to be on your show," Brooke said.

"Right." Krista looked into Brooke's eyes as a smile crept on her face. "Since then there hasn't been anyone I've been interested in until you came walking toward me in the diner. Do you have any idea how sexy you are when you come at a person with purpose?"

Brooke dipped her head shyly. "I've never thought about myself as sexy."

"Oh honey," Krista said, tipping Brooke's chin up with her finger. "You made me imagine things even though I knew you didn't want anything to do with me."

"Who says I didn't want anything to do with you?" Brooke shook her head. "I was walking with purpose because you were sitting there smirking at me."

Krista released a big breath. "Anyway, I was just minding my own business and then you came along and did this," Krista said, pressing Brooke's palm to her chest. "Can you feel how fast my heart is beating? You do that to me, Brooke."

Brooke leaned over and kissed her gently.

"Why couldn't I have met you when I moved to LA?" Brooke sighed.

"It wasn't our time," Krista murmured.

Brooke looked into her eyes and Krista could see the hope, but also a foreboding dread.

"When I came to LA, I got a job I loved with a magazine and was also doing some freelancing," Brooke began. "I met my second husband there. We worked together and spent a lot of time with one another on different projects. and from there we started living together and on a whim got married one weekend. When that fell apart I stopped being whimsical." She laughed bitterly.

Krista squeezed her hands and smiled.

"Before we divorced he'd been wanting to experiment and eventually talked me into going to this party. He had been to these parties before we got married, but I didn't know that at the time. Anyway, there was a lot of drinking and drugs. I kept seeing people go down this hallway at the back of this massive mansion where there were several different rooms. A woman started talking to me and noticed I'd been watching people come and go from the hallway. She was flirting with me hard and heavy, and I liked it, especially since my husband encouraged it." Brooke paused for a moment and took a deep breath.

Krista could tell she was reliving it as her gaze was unfocused. She gently caressed her hand because she could feel Brooke's body becoming tense.

"She led me to one of these rooms down the hall and started kissing me. It brought back all these good memories I had with my girlfriend back in high school. Kissing soft lips and soft touches as her hands glided over my body. It awoke a desire in me that I had locked away all those years ago. We ended up having sex and as we left the room and walked back into the party, a woman walked up to us and confronted her. It was her girlfriend. I had no idea and felt terrible for what I'd done."

"Yeah, but you didn't do anything. You didn't know."

"I slowly slipped away and left them to fight it out. I couldn't believe it. After all these years I was with a woman again and look what happened—someone got hurt. That did something to me, Krista. It made me think that I was being punished. If I was with a woman, something bad was going to happen to her. I'm a little afraid for you right now, even though I try not to believe that anymore."

"Nothing bad is going to happen to me because you kissed me, Brooke. All I felt was good."

Brooke smiled at Krista's reassurances. She looked down to their joined hands. "Later that night the woman's girlfriend pulled me aside. I thought she was going to let me have it, but she didn't. She explained that they had been together for over a year and that her girlfriend liked to prey on unsuspecting women like me. Long story short she wanted me to write an article outing her. She told me how horrible the woman was and the way she'd hurt her. Her words spoke to my sense of righting a wrong and trying to help this woman that I'd played a part in hurting."

"You felt like you were helping her and stopping a bully of sorts?" Krista asked.

"Exactly."

Krista didn't say anything as she processed Brooke's words. On one hand she could see how Brooke justified writing the story, but also outing someone, no matter how bad they were, was simply not done.

Brooke watched Krista and waited.

"I can see why you did it," Krista said slowly.

"It was surprisingly easy to sell the story. I really wanted to write about people in all facets of life; I even have a file that I've kept of stories I wanted to write someday. But after that one story hit I had women contact me with the same types of stories. They were involved with women who were hiding being gay, but they had hurt them terribly in some way. My stories were always accurate because the significant others were giving me the evidence and details. I made myself believe I was helping them. Part of me knew it was wrong, but then another part of me wanted to continue to punish myself for never sticking up for my first love. I thought that these women were bad and I was too."

Brooke sighed and had tears in her eyes. "I know how wrong I was now, Krista. I know it was their story to tell, not mine. And I think that's why I haven't found happiness. What woman would want to go out with me? That's what I deserve for what I did."

"No, no, no," Krista said, each word getting louder. "No one deserves to be unhappy. Yes, you messed up, but we all do, Brooke. You've been manipulated since you were in high school. First by your brother and then by these women that wanted revenge. You were simply their vehicle."

"Thanks for saying that, but I share the responsibility in this."

"You do, but did you ever think if you hadn't written the articles, someone else would?"

"I suppose."

"Not to knock your profession, but there's always some way the story will come out.

"There were a few couples that came to me and thought if they were outed then they could come up with an emotional story on why they hid it. That way the publicity would work in their favor. What's the old adage: any publicity is good publicity."

"Let me see if I heard you right. Some of them wanted to come out?"

Brooke nodded.

"So you write a story that outs them. Then they go on the talk shows and give some heartfelt reason why they were in the closet. All the while they say what a terrible person you are and you get the nastiness and contempt while they play the victim. You get all the malice and they live their lives in the open."

Brooke just shrugged.

"Why do you do that?" Krista asked, disbelieving. "Oh my God! This is more of you punishing yourself," Krista said, obviously upset. "Isn't it?"

Brooke looked away, nodding imperceptibly. "I knew you'd end up hating me."

Krista took Brooke's face in her hands. "I don't hate you. I hate what you've done to yourself. You don't deserve everyone's ridicule, Brooke," she said. She stared for several moments then dropped her hands.

Krista couldn't quite believe everything she'd heard. Brooke wasn't a despicable person. She was writing stories about people who had asked her to do it. Well, most of them anyway. She took a hit to her integrity when she wasn't the one being deceitful, but she never bothered to correct the misconception. Brooke had been punishing herself for years over an adolescent misstep caused by her brother. No wonder she was always stoic and stern, Krista thought. Then a smile played at her face when she realized what a person Brooke had become right in front of her eyes because Krista had finally gotten her to unwind.

"How many people have seen the Brooke I've just spent three days with?" she asked gently.

Brooke's brow furrowed and then she softened as realization dawned. "I don't know that anyone has since that night at the party."

"You're always cautious, serious, and unemotional, just waiting for someone to berate you. And you've done this for years," she said, amazed. "Do you ever take a breath and sit back?"

"When I go home and I'm by myself I can let that Brooke Bell go, but never in public."

"That's why you were so surprised when the group was nice to you, isn't it?"

"Yes. I've never been that vulnerable and open around anyone in years, much less a group of people."

Krista chuckled. "I can't believe this. I knew there was a person that cared about people deep inside you and I was determined to find that person and plead to her not to destroy Lovers Landing." Krista shook her head. "And all this time you were the person who cared enough to take the blame for your supposed victims and write their stories."

"I was never coming here to take it away from you," Brooke said, grabbing Krista's hand. "I wanted to tell you that day in the diner, but I didn't know how."

"Then why did you come?"

There were tears in Brooke's eyes. "Something happened inside me when I heard about this place. I wanted to come here so badly and knew that it wouldn't get out that I was here because no one messed with Krista Kyle's secret lesbian hideout. I knew everyone would keep the secret."

"But you were coming with an escort?"

Brooke scoffed. "That was because your assistant said it had to be couples. I gave her the escort's name so I could make the reservation. I wasn't bringing anyone. I was going to come on my own."

"And then I was waiting on you in the diner," Krista said.

Brooke narrowed her eyes. "Waiting? Are you sure you weren't ambushing me?"

Krista smiled. "Trying to make you an offer you couldn't refuse."

"And then get me into your lesbian lair?" Brooke teased.

"Did it work?"

"Are you kidding me! I couldn't believe my ears. You wanted to spend the week with me at your lesbian resort. How do I say no to that?" Brooke threw her hands up.

"Then why were you so uptight on the plane, and when we got here?"

"Do you have any idea what a nice person you are? I felt like I was deceiving you and I didn't want to do that. There's no way I wanted to hurt you or your place. And when you said I was on vacation I finally gave in and let it all go. You have a way about you."

"So what Brooke am I seeing now?"

Brooke's eyes were unreadable. "I've told you everything about me. How I couldn't stand up for someone I loved and how I've lived with that shame. You know the truth behind the journalist. Yesterday you saw the me that I desperately want to be," she said with tears in her eyes once again. "Krista, you brought out in me someone I didn't know still existed. Someone who wants to be loved, but more importantly, someone that wants to love."

"You're not hiding anyone else in there? Are there any other secrets?"

Brooke shook her head. There was a spark of hope that flashed in her eyes and then they brightened. "Do you remember the favor you asked of me?"

Krista smiled. "I do."

"Can you forget about all of this and be on vacation with me now?" Brooke asked hopefully.

"I can't forget all this, Brooke."

Brooke's face fell.

"I know why you have that sadness in your eyes and I know how to ease it," Krista said, leaning in so they could feel one another's breath. She searched Brooke's eyes and saw the hurt teenager, the tormented wife, the conflicted journalist, and the woman that simply wanted to be loved. She touched her lips to Brooke's and kissed her softly. Then she whispered, "I want you to stop punishing yourself." She kissed her softly again. "You deserve happiness." She kissed her more firmly. "I want vacation Brooke to become everyday Brooke." Her arms wrapped around Brooke and she kissed her with passion, promise and purpose.

16

They were lying on the towel together holding hands, looking up at the clouds lazing across the sky. Their kisses had become heated and passionate until they stopped to breathe. Krista continued to think about what Brooke had told her about the articles she'd written.

"I understand what you mean about holding hands, Krissy," Brooke said, giving Krista's hand a squeeze.

"It's the best, isn't it?" She turned her head to smile at Brooke.

"I wouldn't say the best." Brooke laughed. "But it's up there." She rolled over and propped on her elbow. She trailed a finger along Krista's jaw down her chest and over her exposed stomach. Krista could feel goosebumps where Brooke's finger trailed.

She grabbed Brooke's finger and said, "I feel like I should be mad at you."

"I'm sure there's a list of things you should be mad at me about," Brooke said, intertwining their fingers.

"You never intended to write about my place, yet you came here anyway."

"I didn't know how to tell you why I wanted to come. But then you made it so easy to tell you about my past. No one knows all of that about me, Krista."

"I just knew in my heart that someone must have hurt you. Especially after I met you at the diner; there was something in your eyes," Krista said, rolling over on her side and gently caressing Brooke's cheek. She studied Brooke's eyes and gazed at her face, drinking in her beauty. "You are so beautiful, B. Your eyes have happiness and calm in them now, whereas before there was such turmoil."

"You've made them that way."

Krista smiled. "I should be mad at you for writing those articles and outing those women even if they were horrible." She sighed, stroking her thumb along Brooke's cheek. "Please don't do that again. I know I have no right to ask, but I see you, Brooke. I see the hurt and I see what could be." Krista couldn't hold back any longer. She leaned in and kissed Brooke firmly. She bit down on her bottom lip and then slid her tongue into Brooke's mouth. God, she loved kissing this woman.

After a few moments she pulled back, panting. "I should be mad, but I can't stop kissing you!"

Brooke giggled and then her face turned serious. "The way you look at me makes me feel special, makes me feel like I matter. I want to matter to you."

If she only knew, Krista thought.

Brooke continued before she could respond. "You make the truth come out of me when it would be better kept inside."

"No it wouldn't. You've held all this pain in for so long and what good did it do? You were miserable," Krista said.

"But how could I ever matter to you? The things I've done plus not being honest about this trip."

Krista smiled. "Let me give you some truth. That first night when we were sitting down by the water, the moonlight was reflected in your eyes and it took my breath away. I want to romance you, Brooke. I want to show you that you matter. You matter as a person, but more importantly you matter to me."

"Romance me?"

Krista nodded. "Let's start by going on that sunset boat ride you wanted to take."

Brooke inhaled. "I'd love that. But wait, what if they're doing karaoke tonight? Don't you have to be there?"

"The only place I have to be is with you." Her eyes twinkled and she added, "After all, I'm trying to convince you to keep my resort a secret."

"Wait a minute! Was that your plan all along, to seduce me?" She laughed and then stilled. "And then you'll drop me back in LA and I'll never hear from you again."

Krista scoffed. "You don't believe that. I know it's only been a few days, but you know me, B. This has nothing to do with the resort now. It's all about you and me."

"There's a you and me?"

"I hope so," she said softly.

Brooke blinked and whispered, "It's hard for me to trust."

"I know," she said, running her thumb along Brooke's bottom lip. "Give us a chance?"

A smile toyed at the corners of her mouth and then spread across her face. "I *am* on vacation."

Krista chuckled. "Kiss me."

Brooke captured Krista's lips in a searing kiss. They were a tangle of arms and legs as their lips melded together. Krista couldn't believe how the world fell away when her lips were on Brooke's. And right now all she wanted to do was feel and not worry.

After several minutes of the most luscious kisses, Krista rolled Brooke over. She pulled away and smiled down into Brooke's dark blue eyes. They reminded her of the midnight sky and she hoped they'd be doing this and more tonight. She shook her head. "I can't even think straight around you."

Brooke's eyebrows raised at Krista's comment.

"I did not just say that." Krista laughed. "See what you do to me? I'm hungry," she said, sitting up.

Brooke gave her a smoldering stare.

"Stop that!" Krista said, reaching for their backpacks.

"I'm hungry too," Brooke said, reaching for her.

Krista giggled and held Brooke's roaming hands in her own. "Believe me, I want you just as much as you want me, but we have a romantic night to look forward to."

"I feel like I'm in a dream and I don't want to wake up." Brooke sat up.

"This is a dream for me too," Krista said, squeezing her hands.

"That's really hard for me to believe."

Krista looked at Brooke earnestly. "I know there is not a lot of honesty where we live and in the industry. But I'm telling you the truth, Brooke. You push the bad parts of this world away when you kiss me. And there's so much more I want from you than kisses."

Brooke swallowed and whispered, "I can't wait for tonight."

"Me either." Krista smiled. "Let's eat."

After lunch they swam again and laid in the sun to dry off. Krista told Brooke stories of growing up at the lake with Julia, and Brooke told her stories of happier times growing up in Mississippi.

"I guess we'd better start packing up to go back," Krista said. She grabbed her phone. "Wait."

"What?" Brooke said, sitting back down next to her.

"Smile with me," Krista said, leaning in and taking a picture of them both.

"This has been one of the happiest days of my life," Brooke exclaimed.

"Aw." Krista looked at her phone. "I'd say both our smiles are happy." She showed the picture to Brooke and then said, "Oh, that reminds me. Megan sent me the picture of us from the cliffs yesterday. I forgot to open it. She said it was really good." Krista found the text and opened the picture. "Oh Brooke," she said softly. "Look at us."

Brooke looked at the picture and then at Krista. Neither of them said anything for a moment as they gazed at the picture.

"You're the journalist. How would you describe these two people?" Krista asked, putting her on the spot.

Brooke looked into Krista's eyes and then back at the picture. "If I'm being honest," she began.

"I always want you to be."

Brooke locked on Krista's eyes. "I'm afraid you'll run away if I say."

"I won't."

She took a deep breath. "It looks like two people falling in love," she said warmly.

Krista's eyes sparkled and she smiled. "It does." She kissed Brooke tenderly and then replaced her lips with her fingers. "Don't say anything, please. It's only been a few days and this doesn't make much sense. We're in the middle of a romantic adventure that neither of us expected."

Brooke grabbed Krista's fingers and held them. "Let's see where it takes us. You keep encouraging me to let go and I have. I think it's your turn for romance, too, Krista."

Krista listened to Brooke and could feel the pull between them. This place had to be getting to her. There is no way they could be falling in love! But that's what she'd thought when she saw the picture. *My turn for romance?* This beautiful woman, including her flaws, was being brave and wanted to romance her. If nothing else she'd have a few days of fun and more of those kisses. A smile crept across her face and she nodded.

"Romance, take us away," she said, spreading her arms wide and looking up at the sky. When she looked back down Brooke was grinning.

"Let's go!"

They finished packing up their things and put their clothes back over their now dry swimsuits. Brooke was about to put her helmet back on when Krista stopped her.

"Wait." She grinned and leaned over to give Brooke a quick kiss. Then she put her helmet on.

Brooke did the same and got on her bike. She turned for one more look at this enchanting place that would always have a special place in her heart.

"We can come back," Krista promised.

"We can?"

"Of course. It's our week to do what we want."

"I love this place!" Brooke said, pedaling to the trail. Krista laughed and followed her.

When they came out of the trees and onto the road Krista rode up next to Brooke. "You did great on those hills. You weren't trying to show off or anything were you?" She looked over at her and grinned.

"Hell no! I was holding on for dear life."

Krista laughed. "You looked like a pro."

Brooke grinned at her. "Thanks. This has been so much fun, Krista. Thank you."

"I'm glad you've had a good time. That was the goal."

"And those kisses?"

Krista smiled. She'd be feeling Brooke's lips on hers for a long time to come. "I want more of those." The restaurant came into sight and Krista said, "I'll race you. If I win I get all the kisses I want."

Brooke laughed. "And if I win?"

"What do you want?"

"I want you to spend the night with me."

"Honey, there's no way you're getting away from me now," Krista said. "Ready, go!"

They both started pedaling with all they had. Their laughter filtered on the breeze and Krista pulled ahead. She took a peek behind her and saw Brooke closing in fast.

As they neared the restaurant Krista saw Julia standing outside with Lauren Nichols. She slid to a stop in front of the pair and looked behind her. Brooke came riding up, smiling from ear to ear.

"I won!" Krista said, getting off her bike.

"I guess you've had a good time." Julia grinned, their smiles contagious.

"We did," Brooke said, swinging her leg over and off her bike.

"Hi Lauren," Krista said, catching her breath. "I'd like you to meet Brooke Bell." She waved her hand toward Brooke.

"Brooke, this is Lauren Nichols. She sold us this place."

Lauren's eyes widened when she realized who Brooke was. "It's okay, Lauren. Brooke is my friend,"

Lauren's brow rose, completing her surprised look.

Brooke planted a gracious smile on her face. She was used to reactions like Lauren's, but Krista calling her a friend took the sting out of it. "It's nice to meet you, Lauren."

"Hi," Lauren said, regaining her composure.

"Did you like that little beach, Brooke?" Julia asked with a knowing smile.

"I did, very much," she said, looking shyly over to Krista.

"What are you doing here, Lauren? Come by to soak up a little sun?"

"That's exactly what I'm doing. It's such a beautiful day. I had an excuse though. I brought a couple forms from the Appraisal District for new owners."

"Are you coming tomorrow night for karaoke?" Julia asked.

"I wouldn't miss it," she grinned.

"Lauren can sing," Krista told Brooke.

"Yeah she can," agreed Julia.

"I'd better get back to the office," Lauren said. She turned to Brooke. "It was nice to meet you." She walked past them and waved. "See you tomorrow night."

They watched her drive away and Julia said, "Lauren's had a thing for Krista since high school."

"Oh she has?" Brooke looked over at Krista.

"No she hasn't." Krista glared at Julia. "She's been married since college. She and her husband have raised two great kids and sadly that's all they have in common now. Actually, she sees what a great marriage Julia and Heidi have and that's made her curious."

"Curious as in?" asked Brooke.

"Curious about being with a woman. Not me," Krista added, looking pointedly at Julia.

"Don't kid yourself, Krissy. She'd jump at a chance to be with you," said Julia.

"Too bad. I'm her friend. That's it," Krista said, winking at Brooke.

"I saw that," said Julia. "Is there something you two need to tell me?"

Krista smirked. "Not a thing." She looked at Brooke. "Ready to go to the cabin?"

"Hold up. Don't you want to know how things are going?"

"Things are going great. They're always great when you're in charge," Krista said.

"Don't try to sweet talk me," Julia said. She paused and then said, "But of course you're right."

Krista laughed.

"Everyone has been down at the beach most of the day."

"It's been a perfect day for that," Brooke said.

"What's next for y'all?" Julia asked.

"We're going to wait a little while and then take the boat out. Brooke has requested a sunset tour."

Julia nodded. "It should be a beautiful evening for that. Y'all have fun."

"Oh we will," Krista said gazing over at Brooke then getting back on her bike. "See you later, Jules."

They rode toward the cabin and Julia watched them.

"Krissy's falling in love. You'd better be good to her, Brooke Bell," she said out loud.

17

They were riding by the beach on their way to the cabins when Krista and Brooke both heard their names yelled.

Krista stopped and looked back to see Allison waving at them. They turned around and went back to where they were sitting in chairs on the beach.

"Hey you two," Allison greeted them. "How was the bike ride?"

"It was awesome," Brooke said gleefully. "You should try it."

"Maybe tomorrow," Libby said.

"Could we steal Brooke away for a few minutes?" Allison said, smiling at Krista.

Krista narrowed her eyes at Brooke. "I don't know, she's turning out to be a very interesting date."

"Date?" Libby asked, surprised.

"I did invite her," Krista pointed out.

Brooke sat on her bike grinning, obviously enjoying the attention.

Krista beamed at her because this time yesterday she would've been looking at them warily, not believing their friendliness. Today she was beginning to trust a little.

"I need to walk down and make sure everything is in the boat,"

Krista said, getting off her bike and winking at Brooke. Krista noticed her cheeks had a nice pink tint that wasn't from the sun.

"Okay," Brooke nodded, getting off her bike.

Krista walked down to the boat with the slightest unease in her stomach. She wondered what Allison and Libby would want with Brooke. They had been nice to her so far. Krista was surprised at the sudden protectiveness she felt for Brooke.

"Hey Aunt Krissy," Becca said, bringing Krista out of her thoughts.

"Hey yourself. What are my two favorite girls doing this beautiful afternoon?"

"What we're always doing. Cleaning," whined Courtney.

Krista chuckled. "Everything looks great down here. Good job," she said, stepping into the boat.

"Are you going out?" asked Becca.

"Yeah." She checked the gas gauge and made sure everything was off the floor. For whatever reason the floor was always strewn with shoes, shirts, sunglasses, and other items that people forgot to get out when they came back to the dock.

"Where to?" asked Courtney playfully.

Krista smiled up at her. "I'm taking Brooke out to see the sunset. I thought we'd go over to Costello Cove."

"Ooh, that will be nice from the beach. The sun should be right by the mountain and then fall into the water. Very romantic," Becca added.

Krista looked from one to the other as they stared down at her.

"You're sure showing her a good time," said Courtney.

"I'm trying," Krista admitted.

"So is she your new girlfriend?" Becca asked merrily. "She sure is hot."

"Beauty isn't everything and you both know that."

"We do, but she is and so are you. Plus we saw how you were looking at each other last night."

"When?" Krista asked, stepping out of the boat.

"When you were dancing. It was nice to see you happy, Aunt Krissy," said Becca.

"I'm happy," Krista said, her brow furrowed.

"Not like that," said Courtney as she finished putting away the paddle boards.

"Yeah, and Brooke looked like someone else," said Becca.

"What do you mean?"

"The first day she got here she was all closed off and she seemed scared. But now, she's totally different. We like her. It'd be okay if she's your girlfriend."

"Yeah, we thought she was uptight at first, but not now," added Becca.

"I had no idea you were that interested in my love life." Krista glared at them both.

Courtney laughed. "What love life? You haven't had a girlfriend since we were in middle school. We know you don't sleep around, so..." She held up her hands.

"So, so," Krista said, flustered. She wanted to be mad at them, but instead she laughed. "We're getting to know each other and I'll say this, things aren't always what they seem."

"Go for it, Aunt Krissy! She obviously likes you and look what you've done to her. She's a completely different person," Courtney said, staring at Krista. "And we can tell you like her too," she added softly.

Was it that obvious? She wasn't necessarily unhappy, but Brooke certainly made her heart beat faster. And those kisses. She was always thinking about those kisses. Maybe it was just because no one had kissed her like that in a long time. Who was she kidding, there wasn't anyone she wanted to kiss her like that.

"You know what? I've got to get going," she said, walking past them. "I enjoyed the visit, girls. Toodles." She waved, not looking back.

"Do you think this is what falling in love looks like when you're old?" asked Becca, watching her godmother walk away.

"She's not old," Courtney said, smacking Becca on the arm. "I don't think it matters how old you are. Falling in love makes you happy and do crazy things."

Krista walked back to her bike where Brooke was still talking to Allison and Libby. "I'll meet you at the cabin, Brooke," she said, not wanting to intrude.

Brooke hopped up. "We're finished," she said. "Let me think about it and I'll get back to you if that's all right," she said to the couple.

"That's fine. Have fun," Allison said, waving to Krista.

"We will," Krista said, getting on her bike and coasting away. That uneasy feeling was back in her stomach, but this was not her business. She took a deep breath and let it go. She had a romantic evening with a beautiful woman to look forward to, as her goddaughters had made quite plain.

"You okay?" Brooke asked, riding up next to her.

Krista gave her a big smile. "Yes. I'm looking forward to our evening."

"Me too."

They got to their cabins and as Krista parked her bike and took her helmet off she turned to Brooke and was met by strong hands gripping her upper arms. Brooke was staring in her eyes with an intensity that immediately sent a fire through her body.

Brooke captured her lips in a kiss that began soft and warm and quickly escalated to searing. *My God, this woman's lips are magical*, Krista thought as they pulled apart.

"What have you done to me?" Brooke said, gasping.

Krista raised her eyebrows, not letting her go. "I don't know, but I like it."

Brooke smiled. "I couldn't help myself."

Krista chuckled. She stepped back slowly, knowing if she didn't they'd never get to that boat ride. "We have about thirty minutes before we need to be on that boat. I'm going to shower and change. I'll meet you at the fire pit."

Brooke nodded and Krista walked to her cabin. Good lord, she felt like a horny teenager. She'd kissed this woman and couldn't stop. Her conversation with the girls came back to her. They'd noticed a difference in Brooke and she wondered if everyone else did too. She laughed at herself. "It's only been three days."

She jumped in the shower then quickly dried her hair. They'd be in the boat and wind, so she pulled her thick brown hair back into a high ponytail. After applying a little eyeliner and mascara she dabbed on a bit of lip color and gazed into the mirror. Her blue eyes twinkled with anticipation. She took a deep breath and let it out slowly. "Enjoy each moment, don't rush things tonight," she said to her reflection in the mirror. With a small smile she backed away from the mirror and looked around the room. She walked to the bed and pulled the quilt back, hoping this was where she and Brooke would end up at the end of the night.

Then she went to the kitchen and poured two glasses of wine. With one last look around the room she went out the back door and walked to the fire pit. She set one of the glasses of wine on the arm of a chair and sat down in the other chair.

A few minutes later Brooke walked up. Krista looked her up and down. She couldn't wait to stroke those long tan legs and then feel them around her.

"You're staring," Brooke said with a smirk on her face.

Krista grinned. "I poured you a glass of wine."

Brooke took the glass and sat down. "Thank you," she said, taking a sip.

"After our lake cruise I thought we'd go up and have dinner. We can even dance a little if you want."

"And then?" Brooke asked, looking at Krista over the top of her glass.

Krista smiled at Brooke's question and saw her dark blue eyes smoldering. "What do you want to do then?" Krista asked while sipping her wine.

Brooke took a deep breath and let it out. She smiled and held Krista's gaze. "I want to undress you and slowly kiss every inch of your body."

Krista could feel her cheeks heating up along with the rest of her body. "I told you back at the beach that you matter. I'd like to show you. Believe me," she said, fanning herself. "I hope our night ends like that, but it's not one night to me, Brooke. Don't ask me why because I don't know. I want to share the sunset with you along with a romantic dinner and then walk hand in hand in the moonlight."

Brooke looked at Krista in amazement. "I don't understand it either, but I feel like I have a chance at a new beginning of sorts, Krista."

Krista got up and offered Brooke her hand. "Let's stop worrying about why and trying to understand this. Let's jump in the middle of it."

Brooke took her hand. "And laugh?"

"And laugh," Krista agreed.

"And kiss?" Brooke stood up.

"Definitely kiss," Krista said, planting a quick one on Brooke's lips.

"Let's go."

18

On the boat ride to Costello Cove Krista moved over so Brooke could drive again. The childlike joy on Brooke's face made Krista's heart flutter in her chest. She sat across from her and took in all the nuances of her face. Her smile made little wrinkles around her mouth and she had a hint of a dimple on her left cheek that Krista wanted to touch. Wisps of her golden blonde hair escaped from her ponytail and trailed behind her in the wind. Krista wanted to tuck them behind her ear in the gentlest touch.

She saw Brooke cut her eyes over and immediately turn them back to the water ahead. This view was much better than the one outside the boat, but since Brooke didn't know where they were going Krista brought her attention back to the lake.

"Can you see that little break in the trees and that hint of sand?" she said, pointing ahead.

"Yes," Brooke yelled. "Why were you staring at me?"

Krista reached over and throttled the boat down some so they could hear one another without shouting. "Because you're beautiful."

"Krista…"

"Nope, just feel it, Brooke. All you have to say is?" Krista prompted.

"Thank you," Brooke said, grinning.

"That's right! You're becoming quite the driver. Switch seats with me and I'll show you how to glide up to the beach."

Krista cut the engine and they coasted gently to a stop. She handed a bag to Brooke and took off her shoes. Then she grabbed a soft sided ice chest and stepped carefully out of the boat into knee deep water. Brooke followed behind her and they walked onto the beach.

Krista took a towel out of the bag and spread it on the sand. Then she reached in the little ice chest and opened each of them a beer.

"Have a seat and prepare for the light show," she said, plopping down on the towel.

"It's nice here." Brooke leaned back on her hands and took in the view and her surroundings. "Can anyone come here?"

"On weekends it's usually crowded and during the summer months it is on weekdays too. But we're into September so the season is winding down."

"I'd want to be here every evening if I lived around here."

"Before you ask, I have been here more times than I can count, but always with a group. I have never brought another woman here that I was trying to romance," Krista said, winking at Brooke.

"You know what? It doesn't matter if you have. What's important is that you wanted to bring me here now."

Krista leaned over and kissed Brooke's cheek. "You're exactly right."

They both leaned back and watched the sky change colors. The sun was beginning to fall toward the water. The yellow ball was fading to orange and it began to paint the sky with streams of fire and streaks of red and gold.

"Do you get tired of the secrets?" asked Brooke, taking a drink of her beer.

"I'm kind of in the business of secrets; keeping others' so they can come here and be themselves. But as far as personally, I did get tired of it and that's one reason I came out. I wish it didn't matter to people who you love, but sadly it does. And unfortunately it matters professionally, too."

"Yeah, in a perfect world, no one would care."

"Do you get tired of keeping others' secrets?" Krista asked.

"I don't keep them; I expose them."

"But you keep the secret of how you expose them."

"I suppose I do." Brooke turned to look at Krista. "Allison and Libby are thinking about coming out and approached me to write their story."

"Really," Krista said with a bit of surprise. "Do they want you to expose them?" She wiggled her fingers in air quotes. "Or do they want you to tell their story?"

"I think they want a surprise story like the others."

Krista sat up and faced Brooke. "I know it's none of my business, but please don't do it." She reached for Brooke's hand and took it into hers. "You're a talented writer; don't let them exploit you."

Brooke smiled at her tenderly. "You think I'm talented?"

Krista tilted her head and glared. "You know I do."

"I told them I'd have to think about it. You see, someone has made me reassess my value."

Krista's face lit up. "Is that right?"

Brooke nodded. "I wanted to talk to you about it, but not right now."

Krista's heart swelled with emotion. She leaned in and kissed Brooke. Their lips lingered and then she slowly pulled away. "Look," she whispered, nodding toward the water.

The sky had exploded into bands of color. There were stripes of yellow to orange to red bleeding into deep purples as they touched the dark green of the water.

"Oh my God, Krissy. This is incredible," Brooke said in awe. She scooted over closer to Krista and put her arm around her, pulling her in tight.

They watched as the sky changed colors and the minutes ticked by. Krista felt Brooke kiss the side of her head and enjoyed how she held her pressed into her side.

As the colors began to fade Krista reached up and pulled Brooke's face to hers. "This sky was almost as beautiful as you," she said, gazing at Brooke's lips and then taking them for her own.

"Mmm," Brooke moaned.

Krista swung her leg around and straddled Brooke. She cradled her face between her hands and deepened the kiss. Her tongue stroked Brooke's and pleasure washed over her body. She could feel Brooke's arms around her, pulling her closer. Time seemed to stand still as they explored with their tongues, arms wrapped around one another tightly.

When Krista pulled back slightly and opened her eyes, she lost herself in the dark blue of Brooke's gaze. She took a breath and a smile played at the corners of her mouth. "We really need to get going before it gets much darker," she said, not moving.

Brooke kissed her quickly on the mouth. "Yes ma'am, Captain."

Krista laughed. She got up, grinning at Brooke, and then they both gathered their things.

When they got to the boat Krista pushed it until it was floating on its own. They hopped in and she started the engine and backed them away from the sand. Once they were headed back to Lovers Landing she got up so Brooke could drive.

"Your turn."

"Are you sure?"

"Yes. We don't go as fast on the way back and I'll stand next to you and watch for boats."

Brooke got up and sat in the driver's seat and took the wheel. Krista stood and leaned her hip into Brooke's shoulder. She rested her hand on Brooke's other shoulder and gently stroked back and forth up to her neck. She played with the hair there and ran her nails along the skin. It felt like the most natural thing in the world to do and she breathed contentedly as she looked for boats.

Brooke reached one hand back and caressed Krista's calf for a moment, then returned her hand to the steering wheel.

Neither of them spoke even though they could hear above the

hum of the motor. Both were happy to sink into the comfort of the small movements until it was time for Krista to take the wheel.

She slowly guided them up to the dock, Krista cut the engine and quickly jumped out with a rope to tie them to the dock. After securing both ends of the boat, Brooke handed her the bags and stepped out.

"I hope you found your sunset cruise satisfactory, Ms. Bell," Krista said playfully.

Brooke feigned concentration and said, "It needs one more thing." Then she pressed her lips to Krista's firmly and pulled back smiling. "Now it's perfect."

Krista laughed and took her hand. They walked up to the beach and hadn't noticed Anna and Shelley sitting there.

"Beautiful night for a boat ride," said Anna.

Brooke started to let Krista's hand go, but Krista held on firmly. "It really is. Did you catch the sunset?"

"We did," said Shelley. "It looked like the sky was on fire."

"Brooke, this place looks good on you," said Anna. "I see Krista finally got you to relax a little."

"Thanks Anna. Krista's opened my eyes to a lot of things," she said, smiling over at Krista.

"Good for you both," said Shelley. "Enjoy your dinner."

"Thanks." After they'd walked past them, Krista said, "You tried to drop my hand."

"I didn't know if you wanted them to see us," Brooke explained.

Krista stopped. "Why wouldn't I?"

Brooke shrugged. "Because of who I am."

"I don't care what anyone thinks about me holding your hand. I'm holding your hand because I like to be close to you. It makes me happy."

"I like holding your hand, too."

"Good, because I plan to continue holding yours," Krista said as they began to walk. But then she suddenly stopped. "Don't say shit like that again, Brooke. I'm beginning to know more and more about you and I'm finding out that you're even more beautiful on the inside than this gorgeous face staring back at me."

Krista could see the surprise on Brooke's face, but she continued to look at her sternly.

Brooke's face softened. "Okay."

"Thank you," Krista said quietly and kissed her cheek.

They went inside and Krista chose a table in the corner that was secluded even though no one else was in the restaurant.

After they ordered they went to choose songs on the jukebox. When they sat back down Brooke said, "I'm having the most wonderful time, Krista. Thank you."

"You're welcome. This has been the best day, hasn't it?"

"It has."

"Better than yesterday? You said the same thing last night."

"I'm thinking every day with you is better than the last."

"You're quite the sweet talker, Brooke Bell," Krista said, batting her eyelashes.

Brooke grinned and reached for her hand. They were smiling and gazing into one another's eyes when Becca came bounding up.

"Hey kids," she said cheerfully.

"Hi," Krista said, eyebrows raised, wondering what was about to happen.

"Courtney and I are choosing your songs for karaoke tomorrow night."

"Oh you are?" said Krista. She looked at Brooke. "They like to choose my songs. Sometimes it's scary." She looked back at Becca. "Now remember, Brooke doesn't have to sing if she doesn't want to."

"I remember, but we're going to convince her," Becca said with an innocent smile.

"You don't have to," Krista said to Brooke.

"What if I'm not any good?" Brooke asked.

"Aunt Krissy will help you. Just wait until you hear her sing," said Becca.

Brooke looked over at Krista with raised eyebrows. "Can't wait."

"Why are you still here?" asked Krista.

"Mom, Courtney, and I decided to take a swim after work. We're about to go home."

While Becca was talking, Krista saw Julia walking toward them.

"Hey, how was the boat ride?" she asked.

"It was awesome," said Brooke, squeezing Krista's hand.

Krista smiled at her and then looked at Julia. "It was an incredible sunset. Hey, sorry I was gone all day. I'll come by the office in the morning."

"No problem. It's about time you had a little fun," Julia said.

"I don't mean to take up all your time," said Brooke.

"It's fine. We share responsibilities," said Julia.

"About that. I'll tell you all about it tomorrow, but Brooke won't be writing an article about us. She never was."

"Really," Julia said, shocked. "Well hallelujah."

"I'm sorry if I caused you stress, Julia."

"It doesn't matter. I knew everything would work out. Come on, Becca, let's go home."

"Night Jules. See you tomorrow."

"Y'all have fun now," Julia said in her best Texas drawl.

19

After dinner they strolled down to the beach, hand in hand, and then turned toward the path to their cabins. With the lake on their right and trees whispering in the wind on their left, they walked past the fire pit at Brooke's cabin and down to the water.

"I love the way the moonlight shines on the water," Krista said.

Brooke turned to her and took her other hand and looked into her eyes. "I love the way the moonlight sparkles in your blue eyes."

Krista smiled. "It's not just the moonlight that's causing that sparkle. Let's go to my place."

As they walked up onto Krista's porch Brooke took Krista's hand and pressed it to her chest. "Do you remember this morning when you asked me if my heart was beating fast?"

"I do."

"It still is."

"I hope it's for different reasons."

"It is."

Krista smiled and raised her eyebrows as she tugged Brooke into the cabin. "Would you like a glass of wine?"

"No. I want to remember every moment."

Krista walked over to her and gazed into her eyes. She leaned in and kissed her softly. "Let me show you how much you matter."

She led them into the bedroom. She turned and took the hem of Brooke's shirt and pulled it over her head. Her eyes never left Brooke's as she paused to let her do the same.

Their lips met with more urgency as their hands unbuttoned each other's shorts. Krista stepped out of hers and kicked them aside. She looked up at Brooke with a smirk before her face changed to pure desire.

"Oh Brooke," she said, staring at her lacy black bra and underwear. "You are gorgeous. And you did this for me."

"You did too," Brooke said, her eyes gaping at Krista's deep cut red bra, her ample breasts beautifully displayed.

"Remind me later to ask why you would bring these on this trip," Krista said as she took her finger and slowly ran it along the lace and the delicate skin of Brooke's breast. "Just gorgeous," she whispered again. She could hear Brooke's shallow breathing as she reached around and unhooked her bra.

"As much as I love you in red..." Brooke said, reaching around Krista with one hand and undoing her bra.

Krista raised her brows and instead of saying anything she reached her hand around Brooke's neck and brought her in for a scorching kiss. She started to back towards the bed and their lips never parted.

Krista sat down and looked up at Brooke. Her eyes were dark with desire and Krista watched her lean down and hook her fingers through both sides of Krista's undies. She rose slightly so Brooke could slip them off. She moved up the bed as she watched Brooke take her undies off and join her.

Brooke eased down on top of Krista and kissed her. Their tongues met and began that sensuous dance that drove Krista wild. Her heart beat fast, her skin tingled, and she could feel the wetness between her legs.

She couldn't wait any longer to taste Brooke and pushed her over and settled with her thigh between Brooke's legs. The wetness she felt on her leg enticed her even more. She kissed her way down Brooke's neck and across her collarbone. "Your skin is so soft," she murmured as she continued her path licking around Brooke's rock hard nipple. When she took it in her mouth and sucked, Brooke moaned loudly. Her back arched and her fingers that were resting on Krista's shoulders dug into her skin.

When Krista gently bit down and then again a little firmer, Brooke's moans got louder. It was music to Krista's ears as she kissed her way across to Brooke's other nipple. After giving it a pull and bite she swirled her tongue around it and then flattened her tongue against the pebbly nub.

"Good God, Krista," Brooke said breathlessly while bending one leg.

Krista began to kiss down and across Brooke's stomach, swirling her tongue around her belly button. But when she ran her tongue along the crease of Brooke's outstretched leg she heard her suck in a breath. She made a mental note to remember this particularly sensitive spot.

Now Krista could finally stroke those long, lovely legs. She started with her hand on Brooke's thigh and ran it up to her knee, then down her shin and back around her calf. On the inside of Brooke's knee she left a trail of kisses up to the inside of her thigh. She could hear and feel Brooke's breathing get heavier. Her heart swelled a little knowing she was causing it.

She inhaled Brooke's sexy scent and stopped to marvel at her glistening wetness. With a quick look up she saw Brooke's hands were to her side and her head dug in the pillow. A mix of anticipation and pleasure covered her face. She could see how vulnerable Brooke was, but she also saw trust in her eyes.

Krista looked back down, wanting to give Brooke more pleasure than she'd ever experienced. So she took her tongue and started at her opening and then licked slowly all the way up and around her pulsating clit. Then she explored all of Brooke with soft and firm licks through her folds and around her bud.

When she took all of her in her mouth and sucked, Brooke's

hands immediately found the back of Krista's head and held her there. Krista smiled to herself and sucked a little harder.

"Oh Krista," Brooke said loudly.

Krista loved how vocal Brooke was and appreciated how her fingers were tangled in Krista's hair. She took her finger and teased Brooke's opening then slid inside, quickly adding a second finger, which elicited more groans from Brooke. Krista began a sure rhythm in and out while lavishing Brooke's clit with flicks of her tongue.

"I'm so close," Brooke moaned and Krista responded by pushing her fingers inside and curling them up to find that perfect spot. At the same time she sucked Brooke into her mouth and flicked her tongue.

Brooke came undone, screaming Krista's name. She stiffened and Krista felt Brooke squeeze around her fingers and she almost came right along with her.

Brooke fell back on the bed, her arms out wide and breathing hard. Krista rested her head on Brooke's stomach for a few moments, letting the waves of pleasure run through her. Then she raised up and kissed Brooke tenderly.

Brooke's arms held her to her chest as her breathing slowed. "Krissy," she said.

"Hmm," Krista murmured, smiling at the nickname Brooke sometimes called her.

"What are you doing to me?"

Krista raised up. "Well, I hope I just gave you a really, really good orgasm."

"That was so much better than really good," she chuckled. "That was incredible. I'd tell you it was the best, but you wouldn't believe me."

"I might," she teased.

"You know when you anticipate something and it turns out to be even better than you hoped?"

"Yes." Krista chuckled.

"This was so much better than that!"

"Oh good."

"Words are my business and I can't come up with the right ones because this was so amazing."

Krista chuckled again. "We don't have to talk," she said, capturing Brooke's lips.

After a few moments of another luscious kiss Brooke whispered, "No pressure."

"All you have to do is show me how good I made you feel," Krista said.

Brooke raised up and pushed Krista onto her back. "Good? I've got to work on these words."

Krista giggled. "I like you, Brooke Bell."

Brooke looked down at her with deep dark blue eyes and said, "I'm going to *show* you how much I like you, too."

All mirth left Krista's face and her eyes smoldered at the tone of Brooke's voice. "Then kiss me."

And Brooke did.

* * *

Krista opened her eyes to see the back of Brooke's head. She took a moment to gaze at the different colors of blonde streaking through her hair. She smiled at the gentle ache between her legs. They had shared so many orgasms way into the early morning that she couldn't count. When she looked back on her life she would remember last night as one of the best.

Her arm was around Brooke's middle, holding them close together. She didn't want to think about what was happening between them, but she liked Brooke and liked how she made her feel. She also knew Brooke liked coffee and decided she'd get up and have some ready.

She slowly slid her arm over Brooke's side and then suddenly felt fingers latch onto her wrist. "Where are you going?" Brooke asked sleepily.

"To make you coffee," Krista said, tucking a blonde tendril behind her ear and kissing right below it.

Brooke rolled over. "I don't need coffee; I need kisses." She rolled on top of Krista and brought her lips down.

Krista put her fingers between their lips and said, "Wait. This may be bad morning breath."

"I don't care," Brooke said.

Krista moved her fingers and Brooke kissed her until her heart was beating fast and her breath came in gasps. Brooke pulled back, pleased with Krista's response.

"I was wrong. I need more than kisses," she said with a wicked smile.

Brooke slid down Krista's body and licked her very wet center. "I think you were waiting on me."

Krista ran her hands through Brooke's hair. "You do that to me."

Brooke quickly went to work, swirling her tongue around Krista's clit. "Mmm," she moaned, lapping up Krista's wetness.

Krista knew Brooke's lips were magical, but she'd found out last night that her fingers were, too.

"God Brooke, you are so good at that. Please don't stop," Krista moaned as her hands fisted in Brooke's hair.

Brooke flattened her tongue and then sucked Krista into her mouth. Krista's breathy moans filled the room.

"Yes, yes, Brooke," she yelled and stiffened. The orgasm was quick and intense and blasted through her.

She fell back on the bed. "Good God woman" she breathed. "Good fucking morning."

Brooke laughed where she rested on Krista's stomach. "Can we stay right here in this bed the rest of the day?"

"Mmm," Krista said, tickling the hair at the base of Brooke's neck. She'd become very fond of this sensual little area. She'd driven Brooke wild with her tongue and teeth last night at this very spot. "I have to go over to the office sometime this morning." She looked down at Brooke as her head now rested against her chest. "Can you hear my heart beating?"

"I can."

Krista didn't know what was going on with her heart, but Brooke Bell had worked her way inside it.

"I don't have to go right this minute," she said, raising up and rolling Brooke over.

"Mmm," Brooke said. "Good morning indeed."

20

Krista walked into the bar, through the restaurant, and into the office where she found Julia staring at the computer screen.

"Good morning, Jules. How's my favorite partner?"

"Well, aren't you cheery this morning." She looked at her watch and then at Krista. "It is still morning, barely," she teased.

"Ha ha, very funny." She sat down at her desk and spun her chair to face Julia. "I need to tell you about Brooke. You're not going to believe this."

Julia faced her and put her hands in her lap. "I'm all ears."

Krista explained the articles that Brooke had been writing the last few years.

"Why would she do that? I mean, people think she's evil. Especially gay people."

"You know I told you about what happened to her in high school."

"Yeah. It still makes me mad," said Julia with anger in her voice.

Krista then went on to explain how the first article came about and the others that had followed. She paused to let Julia digest all she'd told her.

"So these women were pretending to be outed and playing the victim while Brooke was the monster. That's just wrong, Krissy."

"I know, Jules. That's exactly what I've been telling her. I'm trying to get her to see her value, her worth. She thinks she deserves all this because she didn't stand up for her high school girlfriend and then because she had sex with a woman who was cheating on her girlfriend."

"So she's punishing herself for something she didn't do and then for something she did do. Well, fuck, Krissy."

"I know. I think telling me all this gave her some relief in a way. She had such a good time the day we went to the cliffs." Krista chuckled. "She couldn't believe the other women were nice to her." Krista looked over at Julia and smiled. "Yesterday was one of the best days I've ever had."

Julia smiled at her. "You looked really happy when I saw you, and then at dinner Brooke couldn't keep her eyes off you."

"I'll never forget last night," Krista said softly.

"Krissy?"

"Jules, what am I doing?"

Julia knew Krista wasn't finished so she didn't answer.

"She's so shy sometimes and then bold. She's funny and has the kindest heart. And those blue eyes; when she kisses me, I never want her to stop," Krista said dreamily. She shook her head. "Good God, listen to me. I'm fifty years old and I sound like a lovesick teenager."

Julia chuckled. "I'll tell you what, Krissy. I still feel like that when Heidi kisses me and if I didn't, why would we still be together? I'll tell you something else, too."

Krista looked up at her best friend with a grateful look. "What's that?"

"I've never heard you talk about anyone else like that."

"What? Sure I have, lots of times," Krista scoffed. Julia shook her head and Krista said, "I know I did with Tara. I was so crazy about her."

"Yeah, you were. But you were young then, Krissy. This is different. You know who you are now, there's no secrets and you know what you want."

"She opened up to me, Jules, and showed me the person she really is without all the secrets."

"Isn't that ironic when our business is keeping secrets?"

"I want her to stop writing those articles. She's a talented journalist and she needs to stop punishing herself. It reminds me of a boxer that keeps taking punches. Somehow they keep standing. She takes punch after punch and thinks she deserves it," Krista said with tears in her eyes.

"While you were trying to get her to value herself, your heart found what it wanted and let her in. It doesn't matter how old you are or how many times you've been in love. You care."

"I do, Jules. I think I did from the moment she strutted towards me in that diner. I had to gather myself and take a breath," Krista said, her heart beginning to pound as she remembered that moment. "What am I going to do?"

"Sometimes we worry so much about what's next we don't enjoy what's now. So you're going to sing at karaoke tonight, dance close with that beautiful woman, and spend the rest of the week having amazing sex. If she does that to you with a kiss I don't need to know the rest." Julia giggled.

"I just want her to be the Brooke I know." Krista looked over at Julia. "She may have the perfect opportunity right here. Allison and Libby have approached her about coming out. She could write a beautiful story about them without all the sensationalism. Of course they'd have to agree to it."

"Would Brooke do it?"

"I don't know."

"Would Allison and Libby?"

Krista sighed. "I can't believe I'm about to say this, but why all the secrets!"

"Get up," Julia said, standing in front of Krista.

She put her hands on Krista's shoulders. "Stop worrying about all this and do what you came here for. Show this woman the best week of her life at Lovers Landing."

"I didn't intend for her to end up in my bed, Jules."

"Exactly. You've both been given some kind of chance here, Krissy. Don't waste it."

"A chance," Krista murmured.

"You've succeeded in getting one of the most closed off people on the planet to open up to you in a matter of days. She's managed to get inside your heart. And right now she's waiting on you at this romantic resort. Why are you standing in front of me?"

"Thanks Jules," she said, hugging her friend. *Maybe Julia was right*, she thought as she left the office grinning.

When she neared Brooke's cabin she could see her sitting down by the water. An immediate smile brightened Krista's face and she felt a flutter in her stomach.

"Whatcha doing?" she asked playfully, dropping the sack of sandwiches she'd grabbed at the restaurant after she left the office. She plopped into Brooke's lap and put her arms around her neck.

"I was just sitting here wondering how I got so lucky."

Krista gave her a huge smile. "I know."

Brooke raised her eyebrows. "Well, tell me."

"Karma can be a bitch and she can be a goddess. I think she's realized that you've had enough of the bitch and it's your turn for the goddess."

"Are you the goddess she sent me?" Brooke asked quietly, searching Krista's eyes.

"Maybe," Krista said earnestly. Then she gently brought her lips to Brooke's for a lingering soulful kiss. "Mmm," Krista moaned as she pulled away, her eyes shining. "Are you hungry?"

"For you," Brooke said, bringing their lips together. When their tongues lightly touched Krista lost her breath and deepened the kiss.

"Wow," Krista said. "I've got to have this," she said, pointing to the sack, "before continuing this." She kissed Brooke again.

"What did you bring us?"

"Sandwiches. And I have the perfect thing to go with an

impromptu picnic," she said, hopping up. "Beer! A Mississippi girl like you should know that. I'll be right back."

While Krista went after the beer Brooke spread a towel out on the sand and opened the sack.

"I didn't realize how hungry I was until I looked in this sack."

Krista handed her a beer. "You should be starving after this morning."

"And last night," she said, wiggling her eyebrows.

Krista laughed as they both dug into the sandwiches.

"While you were gone I did some thinking about the Allison and Libby situation," Brooke said, taking a sip of her beer.

"Oh, and?" Krista bit into her sandwich.

"First, I think it's wonderful what you and Julia have created here. It's such a peaceful, safe atmosphere."

"Why thank you, honey," Krista said sweetly.

"You have people who don't care who knows about their sexuality that come here for fun and then you have those that choose to keep it to themselves who can also come here and be open. But then there's Allison and Libby. They've had such a good time that they don't want to go back to the way they were."

"Is that why they want to come out?"

"I think that's part of it. I need to get more information about their story, but I think I could really make it into something special. A look back in time and then bring it forward to now. Kind of old gay Hollywood meets now Hollywood."

Krista's eyes widened. "What a great idea. You are so talented."

"Thanks," Brooke said proudly and took a bite of her sandwich.

Krista studied her. "Imagine all the stories you could have told. But that's in the past. I hope this is the new Brooke coming forward."

Brooke shrugged. "We'll see. I don't know if they'll go for it."

"It sounds like something they might like. What if they don't?"

"I don't know. I'm still thinking that part through."

Krista didn't want to push Brooke too far. "I'm proud of you, B. At least you're thinking about doing it another way."

She smiled at Krista, reveling in the compliment.

Krista balled her trash up and put it in the bag, finishing her beer in one drink. "Now what was it you were saying about being hungry?" she asked, getting up and swinging her hips as she took a few steps toward her cabin.

Brooke was up and on her in seconds, grabbing her from behind by the waist.

Krista screamed and threw her head back on Brooke's shoulder. "Don't be trashy, B," she said, winking and bending down to grab the sack. Brooke picked up the empty beer cans.

"Race you," she said, taking off running toward the cabin.

Krista whooped and ran behind her.

21

"Do you have a favorite song you want to sing tonight?" Krista asked Brooke as they walked to the bar holding hands.

"No. Isn't this funny—a few days ago I remember asking you if everyone held hands around here and look at me now."

Krista chuckled. "I told you I'm holding your hand because it feels good. It makes me happy."

"There's that word again, *good*. We have to do better. I'm holding your hand because it makes me feel warm and gooey inside."

Krista stopped and looked at her. "That's certainly descriptive."

Brooke leaned in and kissed her softly. "Kissing you makes me feel like I'm on fire."

Krista's cheeks turned pink. "Now you're making me melt. Maybe we don't have to sing tonight after all." She was about to kiss Brooke when she heard Julia yell at them.

"Come on you two. I have drinks waiting for you on the table!"

Krista brought her forehead to Brooke's. "We will pick this up later."

Brooke winked. "Absolutely."

They walked up to where Julia waited. "You have to take a break every now and then," she said, winking at them both.

Brooke's eyes widened. "Don't let her scare you," Krista said, pulling her inside.

Music was playing and Anna and Shelley were on the dance floor. They waved and pointed them to the tables that had been pushed together.

Megan and Renee were looking through the songs for karaoke and Becca and Courtney brought drinks to the table.

"Here," Becca said, setting a drink in front of each of them. "Mom said for you to drink up."

"Okay," Krista said, clinking her glass with Brooke's.

"I've got your songs ready," said Courtney.

"I'm going to need a couple of these before I'm brave enough," said Brooke, sipping her drink. She looked at the pink cocktail and giggled to herself.

Krista leaned over in her ear. "Are you enjoying that Lesbian Licker?" she asked, referring to the pink drink.

"Very much," she replied, her cheeks matching the color of the drink. "Are you reading my thoughts now?"

"Maybe," Krista said charmingly. "Come on, let's dance," she said as a slow song started to play. "I need to feel your arms around me."

Brooke wasn't shy now. She rested her hands on Krista's hips and pulled her close. "I love dancing with you," she said softly in her ear.

"I love it, too." Krista rubbed her hands up and down Brooke's back.

"Can I kiss you?"

"Do you want to kiss me?" Krista said, leaning back so she could see Brooke's eyes.

"Yes."

Krista tilted her head, closed her eyes and waited for Brooke's lips to touch hers. She was rewarded with a soft, gentle kiss. "Mmm, that was nice, B."

Brooke pulled her closer and they swayed until the song ended. When they got back to the table Lauren had joined them.

"Hey Lauren, how are you tonight?" Krista said, hugging her.

Lauren looked at Brooke with a tentative smile.

"Hi Lauren, it's nice to see you again," Brooke said politely.

"You too," she said slowly.

"I can see you're very protective of Krista and I can understand why you'd be leery of me. But I assure you," Brooke said, smiling at Krista, "I'd never want to hurt her."

"Then make sure you don't," Lauren said and then smiled.

"Brooke's a nice person, Lauren. You'll see," Krista said, trying to relieve some of the tension. "Now, what are you singing tonight?"

Before she could answer Becca grabbed the microphone and yelled. "Let's get this party started. We need a singer!"

Renee jumped up and took the mic. She started singing Cyndi Lauper's "Girls Just Want To Have Fun." Everybody cheered and went to the dance floor.

Megan, Anna, and Shelley all took turns. Then Becca and Courtney did a duet.

With the girls still up there Krista joined them. "This one goes out to my two favorite people, Julia and Heidi. Come on, you've got to dance," Krista said as The Emotions dance version of "The Best of My Love" began to play. The girls were Krista's back up singers and the bar went wild.

"Wow, I had no idea you could sing like that," Brooke said when Krista came back to the table.

"We've got a special one for her to do for you later," Courtney said to Brooke.

Krista shrugged and grinned.

The music picked up again when Lauren sang Whitney's Houston's "I Want To Dance With Somebody." The small dance floor was full of sweaty happy bodies singing and dancing.

They all took a break after that to drink and eat some of the food that was delivered to the table.

Krista noticed that Allison and Libby had come in during one of the songs and were at the end of the table. When she looked their way Libby nodded her head and smiled at her. *Please listen to Brooke's idea*, she thought.

"Don't do that. We're supposed to be having fun tonight," Brooke said in her ear.

"Are you reading my thoughts now?"

"Maybe," she said.

Krista could see the emotion in Brooke's eyes and thought she was going to say something else, but then the music began to blare again.

"Come on Brooke," Becca said. "It's your turn."

Brooke looked at Krista with panic in her eyes. When Krista winked at her she could see Brooke immediately calm.

She went to the microphone and looked at the song Becca selected and nodded with a big grin on her face. The intro to "Hit Me With Your Best Shot" by Pat Benatar filtered through the speakers.

Krista watched Brooke start shyly, but then she found her way. The more she listened, she realized this was what Brooke had been living. People kept hitting her, but she got right back up. Everyone sang along with her and if you were an outsider that walked into the bar you'd think this was a bunch of girlfriends having a night out. Brooke wasn't wary or intimidated anymore. She fit right in. Krista felt elation fill her heart because she was sure Brooke hadn't felt this sense of belonging in a very long time.

When the song was over Brooke hurried to where Krista was standing and wrapped her in a hug, spinning her around.

"Maybe you've found a new career," Krista said, laughing and holding on.

"No way! But that was really fun." Brooke beamed.

Allison and Libby took a turn with a duet and then Megan led everyone in "I Love Rock and Roll."

The group came back to the table to get a drink and Becca grabbed the mic again. "I have a treat for you tonight because I am the custom song selector for the uber talented Krista Kyle. If you've never heard her sing, sit back and prepare to be amazed."

Krista took the mic from Becca and said, "Wow, no pressure." Becca had told her earlier what song she'd chosen for her to sing and it was more than appropriate. Dua Lipa's "One Kiss" started and the beat brought everyone to the dance floor. One kiss sure had changed things between her and Brooke, and had opened up possibilities—exactly what the song was about.

She was surprised when Brooke came and danced in front of her. So Krista sang the song *to* her and hoped she listened to the words.

Becca had set it up so Krista went right into the next song which was a breezy tune by Victory, "I Wanna Make You Happy." As Krista sang she realized that in the beginning, when they came to Lovers Landing, she wanted Brooke to have a good time, but now that had evolved to this song. She really did want to make Brooke happy.

These songs coupled with dancing, touching, drinking, and love swirled around the room and created a heady atmosphere that was intoxicating. Everybody was busy eating and discussing what they were singing next when Krista slipped off to the restroom.

She was smiling as she walked through the door and found Megan at the sink washing her hands.

"Having a good time?" Megan asked.

"I think I'm supposed to be asking you that."

"Everyone is having fun. Hey, I wanted to talk to you about something. The thing I like about coming here is that we're away from all the distractions of Hollywood and LA."

Krista chuckled. "That's the whole idea."

"Renee and I have had a chance to brainstorm and come up with some additional scenes for the movie that I think are going to make it groundbreaking."

"Really? I think having a gay couple in it where neither of them dies and they stay together would be so refreshing."

Megan chuckled. "I hear you. There's definitely that, but there's a character that I've decided to expand her role and you would be perfect for it."

"Me?"

"Yep. Are you interested?"

"Groundbreaking, huh?"

"I expect filming to start in about six weeks. I thought you probably weren't as busy during the fall and winter."

"We're not. And I haven't stopped acting altogether since opening this. You do realize that."

"I do. And I can't think of a better actress to play the out and proud lesbian that helps the younger couple through trials and tribulations in my movie. I'm emailing your agent tonight."

"Okay," Krista said, surprised.

"There's a lot of love out on the dance floor tonight," Megan commented.

"Yeah there is."

"You and Brooke seem to be getting along fabulously."

"We are," Krista said guardedly.

"It's none of my business, but be careful, Krista. Brooke makes or breaks careers."

"Why would you say that? She hasn't ruined any careers. Seems to me like those outed women did just fine after."

"I suppose they did, but have you thought about how the community will react if they see you with her? That may not be the best publicity for your career. I know you're not ready to retire."

Krista eyed Megan, hearing what she didn't say as much as what she did. In other words, she had a great part waiting on her, as long as she wasn't with Brooke.

"Thanks for thinking of me, Megan," Krista decided to let it go. She'd wait and see if Megan really did contact her agent with details.

"They're playing Renee's song. I'd better get out there," Megan said, leaving the restroom.

Krista took a minute to be sure she hadn't misunderstood Megan. She hadn't thought past this week with Brooke. She shook her head and decided not to worry about it tonight. She was following Julia's advice and living in the now. And right now she had a captivating woman waiting to dance and sing with her.

22

Krista put her conversation with Megan out of her mind and danced and sang along with the rest of the group. This was by far the most fun she'd had since opening the resort. Lauren even eased up and sang a song with Brooke. Krista knew Lauren was curious and had become a regular at karaoke night. She wouldn't be surprised one day when she went out with a woman. Despite Julia's teasing about how Lauren felt about Krista, she was simply a good friend. Lauren knew she could talk to Krista, ask questions, and not be scrutinized.

Just last week Lauren had told Krista that she and Marcus were separating. She loved him and he was her friend, but she had to take a chance and hoped there was more out there for her. Krista was happy to support her however she needed. At the time she couldn't really imagine finding that with anyone herself and then Brooke appeared in her life. She didn't know where this would go with Brooke, but she hoped Lauren found what she was seeking.

"Come on, Krissy," Julia said into the microphone. "Heidi and I have a special song for you and Brooke."

They walked out onto the dance floor hand in hand. "This should be good," Krista said to Brooke, bumping shoulders.

"Come on everybody." Heidi beckoned the rest of the group.

The first chords of Sixpence None the Richer's "Kiss Me" began and Krista put her arms around Brooke's neck and sang along with them.

"Kiss me," she sang. And Brooke did.

The catchy melody and sweet sounds filtered around the room with the simple lyrics. Krista felt like she and Brooke were wrapped in a soft cocoon of comfort and contentment. As the song ended she pulled Brooke in for a sweet kiss, but then squeezed her tighter with promises of what was to come later that night. She wasn't aware of anything but being in that kiss.

Then the music began again and Krista heard a familiar voice sing the first words of Cher's "If I Could Turn Back Time." She abruptly pulled back from Brooke and looked at the stage. She couldn't believe her eyes. Tara Hollaway was doing her best Cher impression, singing to Krista like she was the only one in the bar.

After the initial shock she realized no one was dancing and Brooke was standing beside her just as confused. She grabbed Brooke's hand and saw Tara follow her movements without missing a word.

Tara was smiling at her now, giving her that bold daring look that usually made her heart flutter for just a moment, but not this time. What the hell was she doing here? Singing about turning back time? Was she making a point? If so she was twenty years too late.

After she sang the last words of the song, she walked directly to Krista and pulled her into her arms.

"What are you doing here?" Krista asked, pulling away, her eyes popping out of her head.

"Saving you from this," she said, nodding toward Brooke.

"What? I don't need saving."

"This so-called journalist isn't going to write one word about your place," Tara said, giving Brooke a menacing look. "Do you hear me?"

"Whoa there, Betty Badass. Brooke is my friend. Don't talk to her like that," Krista said, coming to Brooke's defense. She was surprised once again at how protective she suddenly felt.

"Yeah? Do you always kiss your friends like that?"

Krista was getting irritated now. "What are you doing here, Tara?" she asked more firmly.

"Can we go somewhere and talk?"

"We were having a party," Krista said. She followed Tara's gaze around the room and noticed everyone had gotten quiet and were getting ready to leave.

"I think the party is over," Tara said.

"Way to go, Tara," Krista said. "Hey everyone! The party's not over."

"It's okay, Krista. We were about to leave," Libby said. "Tara," she said, nodding to the other women.

"Hey Lib, hey Allison," Tara said, waving at the couple.

"Well fuck," Krista mumbled as she watched them go and the others follow.

Julia walked over and said, "You always knew how to make an entrance, Tara."

"Julia, it's been too long," Tara said, hugging the woman.

"Maybe not long enough," Julia said, looking over at Krista.

Krista rolled her eyes and then realized Brooke was no longer standing next to her. She whirled around and saw her at the table downing her drink.

"Hey," Krista said, hurrying over to her. "Where are you going?"

"I, uh, I thought you might need a minute," Brooke said, not holding Krista's gaze.

"Are you okay?"

"Krista," Tara said, walking up to them. "Can you please hear me out?"

Krista didn't know what to do. She didn't understand why Tara was there and Brooke looked like she'd lost her best friend. She had to do something.

"Where's Becca?" she said, turning around.

"I'm here, Aunt Krissy," she said, walking over to her.

"Would you please take Tara over to my cabin in the golf cart? I'll be there shortly."

"Sure. Right this way."

"I'll be waiting," Tara said to Krista. She gave Brooke another threatening look and then put her arm around Becca. "Look at you all grown up."

Krista shook her head. Charming Tara was trying to take over the room.

"Why is she here?" asked Julia.

"I have no idea," Krista said, holding up her hands.

"Do you need me?"

"No. She really knows how to clear a room, doesn't she?"

Julia laughed. "Good luck."

"Thanks." Krista turned to Brooke. "Sorry, I should go talk to her."

"Okay." Brooke nodded.

Krista started to walk away and Brooke didn't move. Krista reached out her hand. "Will you walk with me, B?"

Brooke took her hand but didn't say anything.

"See you tomorrow, Jules. Thanks for the song. I loved it," Krista said, looking from Julia to Brooke and smiling. She saw the confusion on Brooke's face and tugged her toward the door.

"I'm sorry about all this. Let me talk to her and see what's going on."

"Okay."

"I can't believe this. I'm just shocked."

Brooke didn't say anything and they were still holding hands when they got to the beach and turned toward their cabins.

"From the words in the song and the way she sang it to you I think it's obvious," Brooke said gloomily.

"What? She isn't here for me, Brooke. I told you we were through a long time ago." Krista was reminded of the last time she saw Tara and how she'd tried to get her to go home with her.

"It didn't seem like that," she said quietly. "I'll stay in my cabin tonight."

"Hey," Krista said.

"I know you need to talk to her and she needs a place to stay, so…" Brooke said, the words running together.

Krista put her fingers to Brooke's lips, stopping her rambling. "I'm not staying with her tonight. Yes, she needs a place to stay. I have an extra bedroom, but I'm not staying with her."

"You're not?"

"No!" Krista said. She looked down and then back up into Brooke's eyes. "I want to stay with you," she said softly.

The relief on Brooke's face was clear and visible as she exhaled.

"Oh baby, I'm sorry," Krista said, cupping Brooke's face. "I thought we had plans for tonight," she said seductively.

Brooke smiled. "I'll wait up."

Krista chuckled. "I won't be long."

She walked Brooke to her back door and kissed her. "I'm sorry Tara talked to you like that. It won't happen again."

"It's okay," Brooke said.

"No, it's not," Krista said firmly. "No one should talk to you like that."

Brooke nodded. Krista took her face into her hands and kissed her tenderly. Brooke went inside and Krista walked over to her cabin. She came so close to blurting out "I love you" to Brooke. Where did that come from? *This night keeps getting crazier*, she thought.

23

Krista walked into her cabin and found Tara in the kitchen pouring them both a glass of wine. Tara smiled at her and handed her a glass. She clinked them together and said, "Here's to us. Because there will always be an us, Krissy."

Krista took a sip of the wine and studied Tara's eyes. Usually when she did this there was a pang of *what could've been* that saddened her heart, but not tonight. That was new.

She'd forgiven Tara for leaving her long ago; back then they were at different points in their lives and couldn't find a common place to be together. She remembered how it hurt and didn't want to go through that ever again.

"Are you going to tell me why you're here?"

"You know, if I *could* turn back time I would've done *us* differently."

"Uh huh," Krista said skeptically.

"Can you imagine? We'd be like Allison and Libby, together for twenty years," she said, smiling affectionately.

"I stopped imagining us a long time ago, Tara. I think it was the second or third different woman you vacationed lavishly with, pictures splashed everywhere, that finally stopped those little fantasies. I could understand all the media coverage because you wanted to be out. What hurt so much was how quickly you found someone else and were so obviously 'in love,'" Krista said with air quotes.

"In love. I haven't been in love with anyone since you," Tara scoffed. "And neither have you," she added, narrowing her eyes.

Krista didn't argue with her because she knew it was true, but then there was Brooke. Something was going on in her heart and Brooke was in the middle of it. "None of that matters now. We've found a way to be good friends."

"As your good friend, what are you doing? Are you seducing this journalist so she'll keep your secrets about this place? Not a good idea, Krista," Tara said, shaking her head.

"Oh please, you know me better than that!"

"From the brief time I saw you with her, your actions spoke volumes," Tara said accusingly.

"What is that supposed to mean?"

"You were all over each other!"

"So was everyone else!"

"But they are married or partners!"

"So what! I like her, she likes me!"

Tara let out a breath and walked into the living room and sat down on the couch. "What's really going on?"

Krista joined her. "Why are you here?"

"I was worried about you. I did some digging on Brooke. She's not who you think she is."

"I know. She's not a threat."

"From what I learned she had nothing to gain from writing an article about your little hold-my-hand hideaway," Tara said sarcastically.

"Don't be like that, it's not a good look," Krista bit back. "No, she never planned to write the article. She wanted to come here, but when I blindsided her with an offer to let me show her what we're really about, she didn't know how to tell me the truth."

"Because she has secrets too, I gather," said Tara.

Krista inclined her head but didn't say anything.

Tara took a sip of her wine and stared at Krista. "And you keep secrets here, so I won't ask."

Krista took a drink and smiled. "If you knew she wasn't writing an article then why did you come here and why did you threaten her?"

"I wasn't sure what she was doing and I didn't want her to take advantage of you," Tara explained.

"Last I checked I can take care of myself."

Tara looked away and then sighed. "I was afraid she might play you like Sylvia did."

"Ugh," Krista moaned. "You had to bring that up!"

"Sorry, but it looks like I may have gotten here just in time."

"Excuse me?" Krista said.

"If you're not seducing her then she's deceiving you," Tara said, but she stopped when she saw the fury in Krista's eyes. "Okay, she's not deceiving you," she said, her voice rising, holding up her hands. "Will you please tell me what's going on then?"

Krista exhaled sharply. "I know this will be hard for you to understand, but we actually talked to one another. The more we talked we began to get to know one another and–" Krista paused to find the right words.

"And?"

"She's not the person you see in the tabloids and on the news."

"Then who is she?"

Krista wasn't sure how much she wanted to share with Tara. "She's been hurt and doesn't think she deserves to be happy. So she's punished herself by writing these articles and pretending to be this horrible sleazy journalist."

"And my dear sweet Krista is trying to heal her, isn't she?"

"More like I gave her a safe place to unload all the self loathing she's been immersed in since high school. And when she did that it was like the real Brooke Bell emerged."

"And this Brooke Bell?"

"This Brooke Bell is someone I really like," Krista admitted.

"But what happens when the vacation is over? Does she go back to LA and her sleazy ways?"

Krista sighed. "I'm trying to get her to use her talents in a way that is nurturing to her soul instead of crushing it."

"I see. And you'd be happy to help her with that nurturing part?"

Krista stared at Tara and rolled her eyes. "Why don't you spend some time with us tomorrow and see what I'm talking about. You'd like her."

"I don't see how. I don't really like people kissing you if it isn't me."

"Oh my God, Tara. Give it a rest. You know you don't care!"

"Actually, I do care. Don't you think I want you to be happy? Because I do. If Brooke is who makes you happy then I'm all for it. I just don't want you to get hurt and there's enough doubt about her that the possibility is real."

"It's not like we're getting married or moving in together."

"I know, but you have to admit this is fast."

"It is, but it also feels really good," Krista said, smiling at the use of that word. She wondered what word Brooke would come up with next. "Look, we've talked enough for tonight," Krista said, taking her glass to the kitchen. "You sleep in here." She walked to the open door at the end of the couch. She turned on the light. "You'll find everything you need. There are towels in the bathroom and extra blankets in the closet." She walked back out and looked at Tara. "I'll see you in the morning."

"You're not staying here?"

"I already made plans tonight," she said with a wink. "I'll see you in the morning, but it won't be early. Toodles." She wiggled her fingers and walked out the back door.

Krista walked slowly over to Brooke's cabin. She couldn't believe Tara had come all this way to make sure she wasn't being taken advantage of. That made two times tonight her budding relationship with Brooke had been questioned. Was it a relationship? What had begun as an exciting day full of possibilities was ending in a bit of uncertainty.

All of that was forgotten when she walked in the back door and saw Brooke. That was the Brooke she knew and that's all that mattered at this moment.

"Hey," Brooke said softly. "Are you okay?"

Krista smiled and walked into her arms. "I am now."

"Do you want to talk?" Brooke held her close.

"Not right now," Krista said, looking at Brooke's lips and then kissing her firmly. "Mm, that's what I need."

Brooke smiled at her, took her hand, and led them in the bedroom.

"What's all this?" Krista gasped as she looked around. There were candles flickering, giving the room a soft glow. Brooke walked over to the nightstand and started a playlist on her phone.

Suddenly Krista heard the music floating around the room. She looked at Brooke and then around the room, confused. "How'd you do that?"

"Courtney brought over a speaker while you were talking to Tara. You have been romancing me the entire time I've been here," Brooke said, walking back over to Krista and putting her arms around her. "You've made me feel special and I don't know how in such a short time it's happened, but there's no one more important to me than you, Krista. Neither of us knows where this will go after this week, but tonight let me show you what I feel for you."

Krista put her arms around Brooke's neck and stared into her sparkling blue eyes. She saw desire there, but more.

"No promises, no commitments. But Krista, you've filled my heart with so many feelings and I want to pour them into your heart so you'll know what you've made me feel." Brooke brought her lips softly to Krista's and took her bottom lip into her mouth. She slid her tongue across it and then into Krista's mouth.

When Krista felt Brooke's tongue against hers coupled with her heartfelt words, she lost her breath and the warmest feeling rushed through her body, making it tingle. If Brooke hadn't been holding her they very well may have ended up on the floor. Krista had had a lot of kisses in her life, but this was one of the most meaningful by far. She could feel Brooke's passion, her tenderness, her want to love Krista. Surely that's what this was though neither wanted to use the word.

Her heart was about to beat out of her chest and her breath came quickly. Krista forced herself to slow down. She pulled her lips away to take a breath and eased her head back. Brooke's lips went to her neck and she trailed her tongue and lips up to nibble her ear lobe and then swirled her tongue around her ear.

"Good God, Brooke. You're going to make me come right here."

"Then we'd better get these clothes off," Brooke said, removing her shirt.

Krista smiled and did the same. They watched one another as they undressed.

There was a directness about Brooke that Krista hadn't seen before. She not only felt wanted, but emboldened. So she climbed onto the bed and settled in the middle, leaning up against a pillow.

Brooke stared down at her from the foot of the bed. Desire was palpable in the room. The music wafted around them and Krista slowly bent her knee and slid one foot up, opening her legs.

Krista could feel her wetness and watched as Brooke gazed down at her with eyes so dark they looked black. Krista couldn't remember anyone making her feel this sexy.

She watched Brooke place one knee on the bed, then the other as she inched toward her. She placed one hand next to Krista's hip and gazed down at her wetness. Then she placed her other hand next to Krista's breast as she continued her trek toward Krista's lips.

Hovering over Krista she looked into her eyes with such intensity that Krista wanted to squirm, but she didn't move.

"The way you look at me, Kris, fills me with such strength. You make me feel valued and I'm not afraid to be vulnerable with you. Let me show you," she said, kissing Krista.

Finally Krista had Brooke's lips on hers. She hooked her arms around her neck and devoured Brooke as her tongue claimed Brooke's mouth. This woman not only made her feel sexy it came with such an intense want that she needed Brooke's hands on her now.

Somehow Brooke knew just what Krista wanted and needed. She tore her lips away and began to tenderly kiss down Krista's neck across to her shoulder. Then she bit down and Krista yelped with surprise. She ran her hand through Brooke's hair and watched her kiss down and around her pebble hard nipple. Her tongue swirled and teased and then found the sharpened point of her nipple.

Krista groaned when Brooke sucked it into her mouth. "Oh baby, yeah," she exhaled.

Brooke bit down and held her nipple there as she flicked her tongue over the sensitive tip.

"Fuck, B. That feels amazing," Krista exclaimed. Where they'd had sex before, this felt like a whole new level. Her hands were buried in Brooke's golden locks as she took her skilled mouth over to Krista's other breast.

"You are so beautiful, Krissy," Brooke said as she continued her journey across and down Krista's body. When she swirled her tongue around Krista's belly button she arched her back. *She's getting closer and closer to where I need her*, Krista thought as she panted, her breath coming quickly again.

Krista had one leg draped over Brooke's lower back as her other fell to the side.

"I need you, Brooke. Please," Krista pleaded.

Brooke put one arm under Krista's bent leg and her other hand splayed across Krista's stomach. She looked up at Krista and could see the want and need in her eyes.

"I want you, Krista," Brooke moaned and licked the length of her wetness.

"Oh Brooke," Krista yelled as her hips bucked.

Brooke's tongue licked up and down and swirled around Krista's hardened nub. Then she teased her tongue around Krista's opening. She pushed inside and Krista moaned, "Oh baby, baby," and her hands flew to her side as she fisted the blanket.

Brooke replaced her tongue with her fingers and sucked Krista's clit in her mouth. The sensations made Krista raise off the bed again and moan.

"Fuck Brooke, that's so, so..." she groaned loudly.

Brooke's fingers began moving in and out and their magic brought Krista closer and closer. As much as she wanted this to last and last, Krista couldn't take anymore. She reached down and found Brooke's chin and pulled her up.

"I've got to have your lips here," she said, crushing her mouth on Brooke's and wrapping her arms around her neck. She was so close and Brooke pushed in deep and curled her fingers up.

Krista saw stars behind her eyes and wrestled her lips from Brooke's. With her arms and legs wrapped around Brooke, she screamed as the orgasm took her. It rolled up and down her body and she held tight, relishing every juicy moment.

Her legs fell back on the bed and her body followed. "Oh Brooke," she moaned. "That was–"

"Don't you dare say good," Brooke said before Krista could finish.

Krista chuckled. "I wasn't, I promise," she said, still panting. "Look at me," she said softly. Brooke pulled back and her eyes met Krista's.

Krista cupped the side of Brooke's face. "That was amazing. I felt what was in your heart."

"You put it there." Brooke smiled.

"You're going to have to give me a minute. That was just incredible."

"It's okay," Brooke said, resting her head on Krista's chest.

Krista stroked her back, "Baby, baby, baby. You made my body sing." She took a few deep breaths, simply enjoying lying with Brooke like this.

"You said I give you strength. You make me feel beautiful," Krista said, still stroking Brooke's back.

"What?" Brooke said, confused. "You're always one of People Magazine's most beautiful people."

"People tell me that all the time, Brooke. But you make me *feel* beautiful. There's a big difference. I can see how beautiful I am in your eyes. It's the way you look at me."

"You are," Brooke whispered.

"And so are you," Krista said, sitting up and rolling Brooke over. "Can you see it in my eyes? I see inside you. I see your heart and it's beautiful. It's not what you let other people see, but I see it."

Krista placed her lips on Brooke's and showed her how beautiful she was.

24

Krista's eyes fluttered open and for a moment she floated in absolute bliss. She felt a hand gently stroke up and down her back. Her head was resting on Brooke's chest and one arm was draped over her middle.

"Mmm, I could get used to this," Krista whispered. Then with her voice low and thick with sleep she said, "Good morning."

"I didn't mean to wake you," Brooke said, cuddling her close.

"You didn't. Have you been awake long?"

"For a while."

"Why didn't you wake me?" Krista turned her head to kiss Brooke's chest.

"I was burning this moment into my memory."

Krista chuckled. "Last night before we fell asleep is burned into my memory."

"Wow," Brooke stated.

"Yeah it was," Krista agreed.

"I've also been thinking about Allison and Libby."

"Oh," Krista said, raising her head to look into Brooke's eyes.

"I thought I'd go over there this morning and tell them my vision for their story."

"Is it what you told me?" Brooke nodded. "I'm proud of you, B. I can't imagine them not liking your idea."

"We'll see. I'm not exactly the person they expected me to be."

Krista smiled into her eyes. "I really like this Brooke."

Brooke gave Krista a half smile back. "But I am that other person too, Krista."

"I think you've wanted to be this Brooke for a long time, but couldn't stop punishing yourself. You don't have to do that anymore. You see that, right?"

"I do. I want to be this person that's with you. But for a long time I've felt unworthy and less than. That doesn't change overnight."

"I understand that. But baby," Krista said, cupping the side of Brooke's face. She looked into her eyes compassionately. "Don't ever think you're not valuable. You are to me."

"You make me feel like I can do anything," Brooke whispered.

"You can."

"Enough about me. What are we doing today?" Brooke asked, taking a deep breath.

"I had a place I wanted to show you on the paddle boards. And then I thought we'd go for a boat ride. We can invite Tara, Allison, and Libby if that's okay with you."

"You never did tell me about your talk with Tara."

"She doesn't know the Brooke I do. That's why I thought she could go with us."

"Oh, so she came to rescue you from the evil journalist."

"Something like that." Krista smiled and kissed Brooke softly. "Do I need saving?" she whispered seductively.

"Your secret's safe with me."

Krista pulled back. "My secret? Do you think you're a secret?" She tilted her head. "*We're* a secret?"

"Aren't we?"

"Not at all." They hadn't discussed what happened after the week was over, but Krista certainly didn't want things to end there. "I know this all started as a vacation, but is that where you want it to end?" she asked nervously.

"No," Brooke said.

"I don't either."

"So much has happened in such a short time, Krista. It's scary and glorious and overwhelming," she said, her eyes growing bigger with each word.

"I know, I know," Krista said, quieting Brooke with a gentle kiss. "Let's take a breath. We don't have to decide anything right now. We still have a couple of days. But you're not a secret. Not now, not ever. Okay?"

"Okay," Brooke said, kissing her back.

"I don't know about you, but I'm hungry," Krista said, sitting up. "Don't answer, I know you're always hungry for that," she said, winking. "Let's shower and then have breakfast. While you're talking to Allison and Libby I'll get our paddle boards ready." Krista got up and walked to the bathroom. At the door she turned around and said with a naughty grin, "Are you coming? I said I'm hungry."

Brooke jumped off the bed and joined her.

* * *

Krista had two boards, paddles, and life belts waiting on the beach. Brooke had been at Allison and Libby's for quite some time and Krista hoped that was a good sign. A horn honked and got her attention as she looked back toward the restaurant.

She recognized Lauren's car pulling up to the beach, so she waved and walked up to meet her. Lauren got out and walked around the car.

"Hey Krista," Lauren said as she walked to the sand.

"Hey yourself. Is it a sun day, fun day?" Krista asked, grinning.

"It is. I had so much fun last night at karaoke I decided to take the day off."

"Good for you. It was a fun night. Well, until it ended so abruptly."

"Did you know Tara was coming?"

"Not at all."

"It was surprising." Lauren chuckled.

"You can say that again."

"I've noticed you and Brooke seem to be getting quite close. I'm sorry," she said, holding up her hands. "That's none of my business."

"It's okay, Lauren. We have found an unexpected and rather amazing connection."

"Good for you!"

Krista chuckled. "Yeah, good for me."

"What have you done now?" Tara asked, walking up.

"Just being my amazing self, Tara. You know," Krista said with a wink.

"Okay, I deserve that," Tara laughed.

"Tara, this is my friend Lauren. I'm not sure you got to meet her last night."

Tara tilted her head and reached out her hand. "I did not. It's very nice to meet you, Lauren." She held Lauren's hand. "I was focused on saving my friend from a disaster and didn't get to meet anyone."

Krista watched Lauren's face. It went from starstruck to amused and she thought, *Tara would be the last person I'd let anywhere near Lauren.*

"Why? Your friend is more than capable of taking care of herself. I'd have thought you knew that, Tara. It is so nice to meet you, though," Lauren quipped back.

Krista stifled a laugh as a smile grew on Tara's face. Perhaps she needn't worry about Lauren after all.

"You're absolutely right. I was corrected about that last night," Tara said, bowing her head at Krista.

"As much fun as last night was, I'm hoping we'll do it again tonight. How about it, Krista?" Lauren asked.

Krista laughed. "I'm sure someone will be singing."

"Come on, you know how we love to hear you sing," Lauren coaxed.

"We'll see. Right now, I'm waiting on Brooke. We're going paddle boarding."

"Paddle boarding? No thank you," Tara said with a frown.

"You can stay right here and enjoy the beach. I'm sure Becca will be glad to bring you drinks," said Krista.

"That sounds heavenly," said Lauren.

"Here you go," Krista said, gesturing to two chairs facing the water. She saw Brooke walking toward them and grinned.

"Good God, Kris, can't you control yourself?" Tara said, feigning disgust.

Krista laughed, knowing she was teasing. "Hey babe," she said, kissing Brooke just to get under Tara's skin. The surprise on Brooke's face was adorable.

"Please, lovebirds, don't let us stop you," Tara said. "Shall we?" she said to Lauren.

Lauren walked over to the chairs with Tara, chuckling at the exchange.

"Tara, we'll take you on a boat ride this afternoon. Toodles," Krista said, leading Brooke to the paddle boards.

When they were far enough away that they couldn't be overheard Krista asked, "How'd it go?"

"I think it went well. They listened and asked a lot of questions. I explained to them that I didn't really want to be that journalist anymore and they seemed to understand. When I outlined my idea and expressed the impact I thought it could have, that really got their attention."

Krista beamed. "Good for you." She wrapped her arms around Brooke and gave her a hug. "I'm so proud of you."

"You keep saying that. Why?"

"Because standing up for yourself isn't easy. Doing something new is hard and you've taken the first step."

"If you say so. Thanks. Let's paddle."

"I say so," Krista winked.

They got on the paddle boards and glided away from the shore. Tara and Lauren applauded them and waved. Krista led them around the dock and past the little beach that was behind Brooke's cabin. The wind was calm, so the water was smooth which made for easy paddling.

"This is perfect, Krissy," Brooke said as they paddled next to one another.

"I ordered this weather just for you."

"You are so good to me. Thank you."

"Good? There's that word again."

Brooke laughed. "You make me happy."

"You make me happy too, B."

They paddled a little further and then a small inlet opened up to their left.

"This way," Krista said. After they'd paddled away from the main part of the lake Krista said, "Does this look familiar?"

Brooke paddled up next to her and looked ahead. "Is that the beach we biked to the other day?"

"It is!"

"How cool! It took us almost an hour to ride to it and less than twenty minutes to paddle here."

"Yep. You have to know it's here or you'll miss the inlet when you're riding by on a boat."

"Can we stop?"

"Of course. That's why I have a bag on my board."

They glided into the shore and their boards bumped up to the sand. Krista grabbed the bag and left her paddle on the board. She took out a towel and spread it out for them.

Brooke grinned and plopped down on the towel. "What else is in that bag of yours?"

Krista chuckled. "Just water. Here," she said, handing her a bottle.

They stretched their legs out in front of them and enjoyed simply being together.

"Have you been in love?" Brooke asked.

Krista stared out at the water. "I have. Twice."

"Twice?"

"Yes. There were a couple of times I thought I was, but really there were only two. I was in love with Tara and then one summer when I was working here."

"What? Tell me," Brooke said, keenly attentive. "Please."

Krista smiled. "There was a single mother that spent the summer here with her two daughters. I fell hard and fast. I was in college and almost transferred to a school near her, but it wouldn't have been a good idea. She could see that," Krista sighed. "She said it wasn't our time. Anyway, we had a glorious summer and she's still very special to me."

"That's such a sweet and sad story."

Krista shrugged. "Your turn. How many times have you been in love."

"That's such a hard question for me. I think it was like you said, there were times I thought I was in love." Brooke sighed and continued. "I was in love with my high school girlfriend. I know it doesn't seem like it with what I did, but I was crazy for her. But I was also a coward."

"Brooke," Krista started.

"I know, I know." She nodded. "That's how I feel, Krissy. I understand what you said and I'm trying. Okay?" Krista nodded. "As I told you, I loved my first husband, but wasn't in love. I'm not sure I even loved my second husband."

"Was there someone else?"

"No. I can't trust myself. I'm not sure I know what being in love feels like."

Krista looked over at her with such tenderness in her eyes. "You've given me a look at your heart, Brooke. I think you can trust it as long as you stop trying to hurt it."

Brooke met Krista's eyes. "When I look at you or think of you, my heart hurts."

"It hurts!" Krista said, shocked.

"In a good way," Brooke quickly reassured her. "It feels..." She sighed and shook her head.

"What? Tell me."

"I'm afraid to. I'm afraid it will be too much."

"It won't be," Krista said, grabbing Brooke's hand. "Tell me what's in your heart."

"When I kiss you, when I touch you, when you touch me my

heart races but it fills up and empties and fills up again. Of course it feels amazing physically, but it's more than that." Tears pooled in Brooke's eyes. "It feels like you pour love into my heart and then my love empties into you and then it fills up again. And this goes on and on."

"Oh Brooke," Krista said, cupping her face with both hands. She kissed the tears that trickled down her cheeks. Krista felt her heart swell. She understood what Brooke had described because she felt it too. She was just as afraid as Brooke was for several reasons, but none of those seemed to matter at this particular moment.

Krista stared into Brooke's eyes as the tears faded. "I feel it, too." She softly pressed her lips to Brooke's and kissed her with the love she felt in her heart.

Brooke wrapped her arms around Krista and they both sank into the kiss. Krista felt her heart fill with Brooke's love and then she gently nudged her tongue between her lips and kissed her love into Brooke's heart.

This kiss was all that mattered: it softened for moments and then heated up all over again. It was a kiss of newly professed love, but certainly not the first between them. This love was there almost from the beginning, but they were both unbelieving, afraid, and hesitant. But that didn't stop them from finding their way and discovering just what was in their hearts.

Brooke slowly pulled back and looked at Krista with such love. "There's something about this beach."

Krista chuckled. "There sure is."

"It's our beach now."

Krista smiled. "I'm just as afraid as you are. I know I act like I have it all together, but I don't. What I know is that you make my heart happy. When I see you, when you smile at me, my heart fills with happiness and I like it."

"I love you, Krista," Brooke said.

"And I love you."

25

They held one another, letting their love surround them. Neither said anything, both simply soaking in the newfound feeling and letting their hearts do the talking.

Brooke pulled back and said, "How did this happen so fast?"

Krista leaned back propped on her hands. "I've actually been thinking about this. I think deep down I created Lovers Landing because my heart was looking for you. I still had hope there was a happily ever after somewhere for me, but since I didn't have it I wanted to at least give others a sense of it when they came here."

"Looking for me?"

Krista shrugged. "Yeah, it's you. My heart knew it from the moment you walked in that diner. I'm telling you, Brooke. No one has ever made my heart stop like you did that day. I didn't realize it then, but my heart knew."

"I get it. When I turned to see who the waitress said was waiting on me, our eyes locked and it was as if some force was pulling me toward you. That's why you thought I was strutting. I couldn't help it," she said with a smile growing on her face.

"Our hearts connected right then and we've been trying to catch up ever since," Krista said, leaning over and putting her head on Brooke's shoulder. "You're the person my heart's been waiting on all this time."

Brooke laid her head on Krista's. "I want to be your person," Brooke whispered.

"You are," Krista said quietly.

"It's like this, Krissy," she said, sitting up so she could face her. "For as long as I can remember I've been barely keeping my head above water. Someone would always come along and push me under and then I'd struggle just to get a breath. Of course I caused it. I stayed quiet and let my brother and his hate push me under. Then trying to pretend I was like everyone else and getting married pushed me under again. I made it back above water when the articles started and since then I've been under and grabbing a breath in between." Brooke sighed and continued. "When you offered to let me come here it felt like taking a breath. When I got here it felt like you were holding me up and as I began to breathe I didn't go back under. Now I feel like I'm floating; we're floating in this together."

"I've got you, baby," Krista said, squeezing her hands.

"It's hard to believe this is real, but my heart tells me it is. I'm not struggling any longer. I wanted to tell you last night, but I was afraid it was too much."

"You did tell me in your way. You showed me, Brooke. Last night wasn't just sex. I felt it and you felt it too. It was magical. I didn't want to go to sleep."

"I know." Brooke giggled. "When I woke up this morning and you were in my arms I wanted to stop time."

Krista smiled. "That's not the only time it's going to happen. I want to wake up next to you, on you, you on me…"

"I get the picture," Brooke said, interrupting Krista, but then her face fell.

"What's wrong?" Krista asked.

"You do realize it's not going to be easy for you," Brooke said, her voice sad.

"Just stop right there. No more torturing yourself. Let's enjoy these last couple of days and be in love! We'll let the world in later. Okay?"

Brooke's face lit up with a smile. "Okay."

"We'd better start back. I did tell Tara we'd take her on a boat ride after lunch."

"We've got time for this, don't we?" Brooke said, bringing her lips to Krista's.

"We've always got time for this," Krista said, her lips poised against Brooke's. "I love the way you kiss me." Brooke claimed Krista's lips as her arms pulled her in closer.

Krista moaned and pushed Brooke back on the towel until she was on top of her. Their kisses were hot and wet and luscious.

"I thought we needed to go," Brooke murmured as Krista tugged on her earlobe.

"I needed you more," Krista said softly, kissing Brooke again.

She finally pulled away and looked down at Brooke. "I get lost in you sometimes, B. I love you."

"Oh, I love you, Krissy. And I love hearing you say that."

Krista grinned. "You'll be hearing it a lot more, but now we must paddle, my love." Krista got up and pulled Brooke with her.

Krista secured her bag to the board and looked over at Brooke who was already standing on her board ready to paddle. She took a moment and stared, taking her in.

"What are you staring at?"

"The woman I love. Do you want to know what I love?"

"Sure."

"I love that she's good to herself, and honest, and loves me back."

"I'm learning to be good to myself, but loving you is the absolute best," she said, her face full of love.

Krista stood on her board and began to paddle back to the main lake. Brooke was in front of her and she had a wonderful view of this gorgeous woman. She couldn't help but wonder about Allison and Libby. Surely they'd like Brooke's idea for their story. And if they didn't, who cared. Brooke wasn't writing those kinds of stories anymore. Krista's heart was full.

* * *

After lunch Krista and Brooke walked to the dock to get the boat ready. Allison, Libby, and Tara all went to their cabins to change and then meet them there.

Krista held Brooke's hand as they stepped onto the walkway. She bumped shoulders with Brooke. "You don't have to help me."

"I want to. Who knows, this could be my job someday."

Krista laughed. "Do you want to be my First Mate?"

"I do, captain. Just tell me what to do."

"Keep that in mind when we get back to your cabin tonight," Krista said seductively.

Brooke chuckled then leaned over and kissed her on the cheek. "I love you."

Krista giggled. "I love you too."

"You're acting like a couple of silly kids," Courtney said as they reached the boat.

"Courtney dear," Krista said. "Do you remember being a silly kid?"

"Yeah. It wasn't that many years ago."

"Did you have a lot of fun?"

"Well yeah, now that you mention it, I did," she said, chuckling.

"Call me a silly kid all you want because Brooke and I are having a really good time. Aren't we?" Krista said.

"We certainly are," Brooke said, wiggling her eyebrows.

"Another life lesson from my awesome Aunt Krissy. Thank you," Courtney said earnestly.

"You are welcome. Do you want to go with us? We're going over to the backside of the cliffs to swim." Courtney considered her offer. "You can drive," Krista added.

"I can?"

"Yes ma'am. I want to sit in the back with my girl," Krista said, winking at Brooke. "You can show Tara how to drive. She gets off on control."

"I know you just said that with love," Tara said, walking up.

Krista turned around, grinning. "You know I did."

"There's nothing wrong with being in control."

"I couldn't agree more," Krista said, glancing over at Brooke.

"Here we are," Allison said, waving to them. Libby followed close behind.

Krista and Courtney quickly finished putting supplies in the boat while the others looked on chatting.

"Okay. Libby and Allison, y'all can take the front," Krista said, holding their hands while they stepped into the boat.

"I just love that little Texas accent of yours slipping out occasionally, Krista," Allison said, stepping to the front.

"Tara, you sit in the co-pilot's chair and if you're nice, Courtney will let you drive."

"Krista, honey, you know I'm always nice," Tara said, taking Krista's hand and stepping into the boat.

"Come on, gorgeous. You're with me," Krista said, holding her hand out to Brooke.

She pushed them away from the dock as Courtney started the motor and they glided away.

Krista sat in the back and pulled Brooke down next to her.

"Does anybody want a drink before we speed up?" Krista yelled to the group. When no one said anything she said, "Okay, Courtney, hit it!"

Courtney pushed the throttle down and off they went. Krista leaned back and put her arm around Brooke's shoulders. The wind whipped through her hair and the smile grew on her face. *This is the life*, she thought: her arm around the woman she loved, the wind in her hair, flying over the water and off to a beautiful little spot to swim.

Brooke turned around and looked at her, reading her thoughts. She leaned in and shouted, "You look beautiful!"

Krista's eyes sparkled. "I feel beautiful!"

As they neared the cliffs Courtney motioned Tara into the driver's seat and gave her instructions. Tara took the wheel and drove them around the cliffs. They slowed down and Courtney killed the engine.

"Is this okay, Aunt Krissy?"

"Perfect." Krista jumped up to put the anchor out and Brooke helped her unroll the swim pad.

She gave everyone a lifejacket and they began to jump in the water.

"Aw, this is wonderful," Allison said after she jumped in and came back to the surface.

Courtney and Brooke jumped in and joined her.

"Drinks?" Krista yelled. She threw a beer to Brooke and Allison then reached back in the ice chest and grabbed a soda for Courtney.

"I'll take one," said Libby. Krista handed her one and then did the same for Tara.

"So you and Brooke seem to be getting along," Libby said.

Krista looked up at her and laughed. "Yeah, you could say that."

"Aren't they cute," Tara said. Krista took Tara's beer and pushed her in the water. Tara came up laughing.

Brooke threw the unopened beer to her. "How cute am I now?"

Tara continued to laugh and floated over to the others.

"When we came to your house that night I certainly didn't see this coming," said Libby.

"Me neither. No one is more surprised by all this than I am, Libby. I assure you. But you know what, fuck it. She is not the person we all thought."

"I don't know."

"I do. She told me about her idea for you and Allison. Honestly, it sounded amazing. Imagine the good that would come from it."

Libby nodded. "I know. I liked it, but Allison has reservations."

"Why?"

When Libby didn't answer Krista said, "Oh wait, I get it. She doesn't want her legacy to be about coming out and changing Hollywood. She'd rather people value her talent and her work."

"Exactly."

"I can't imagine people overlooking her talent. It doesn't seem possible," Krista said. "Yours either for that matter."

"I was surprised Brooke suggested it."

"She's trying to find another path. I think you'd agree she is a talented journalist."

"I do. That's why we approached her."

"I hope you'll talk to Allison. Imagine the roles you two could create." Krista said.

"The other night Megan mentioned a role she has for you, but she made me think that it wouldn't be there if Brooke was still around. Have you thought about what this relationship could do to your career?"

"You know, I don't usually talk about parts with other people when it's in a setting like this because you never know if the director means it."

Libby chuckled. "That's true."

"But she did tell me about it and implied the same thing."

"So what are you going to do?"

"Nothing. I'm not giving Brooke or anyone else up for a part. I don't care how good it is. Maybe it would be the perfect part for you or Allison."

"I don't know, Krista. We agreed a long time ago that we'd come out when we were both ready. We're ready and we agree on Brooke, just not her new approach. So, we're considering both and letting her know tomorrow."

"Hey babe! Aren't you coming in?" Allison called to Libby.

"On my way, honey."

"Come on, Krissy. The water's perfect!"

"Go have fun with Brooke, she's crazy about you," Libby said.

Krista turned to Libby, her face sincere. "I'm in love with her, Libby."

Libby smiled. "No judgement here. I fell for Allison the first time we met, but be careful. It's going to take more than one article to change Brooke's reputation."

"I'm not as concerned about her reputation as I am with her. She's been hurt enough."

Libby nodded and walked to the back of the boat. "Hold my beer."

Krista held it while she jumped in and then handed it to her. She hoped Libby could convince Allison, but if she didn't, they'd figure it out. As she looked down at Brooke and saw the love in her eyes she felt like they could do anything.

"Yeehaw," she said, jumping in and landing with a big splash.

26

When they got back to the dock they went their separate ways, planning to meet at the bar later for dancing and karaoke.

"Hey Tara, I meant to ask you earlier. Where did Lauren go? I thought she was spending the day," said Krista.

"Something came up at work, but she's coming back tonight. We're singing together," Tara said, grinning.

"Listen Tara, Lauren is a nice person and good friend. Take it easy on her," Krista warned.

"What do you mean? She's the one that's interested, Kris."

"Look. I'm sure she is interested, but Tara, I'm asking you to go easy. She's just separated from her husband of twenty-five years. She's curious, but also fragile."

"Come on, Krista. I'm not like that anymore."

"Really? You do remember last week at the benefit. You were there with someone and asked me to go home with you."

"I'm always going to ask you to come home with me. Well," she said, looking over at Brooke, "not anymore. I do respect your relationships."

"But what about the woman you were with?"

"That was the second time we went out. And she didn't go home with me. Believe it or not my reputation isn't necessarily accurate. I'd think you'd understand that with all that's happened this week," Tara said, obviously referring to Brooke.

"I do, but I also know you. And you can be very charming and you're always beautiful. That's a deadly combination."

"Why thank you. I'll see you tonight," Tara said, walking away from the dock.

Krista shook her head and watched her leave. "Never a dull moment with that one."

Brooke chuckled. "You're both quite entertaining."

"Is that so," Krista said, quickly turning around with a smirk on her face.

"It is. Come on sweet cheeks, I'll walk you home," Brooke said, weaving her fingers through Krista's.

"Sweet cheeks?"

"Everyone says babe. Words are my thing. We'll see what else I come up with," she said, wiggling her eyebrows.

Krista chuckled. "This is going to be fun."

"Yeah it is," Brooke said, kissing her quickly and leading them down the walkway.

Krista was swinging their hands and grinning at Brooke when she kissed the back of her hand and said, "I think you're beginning to understand why I love holding hands so much."

"I never knew something so simple could feel so amazing. It fills my heart when you take my hand."

Krista knocked shoulders with her and beamed. "I feel it, too, B."

"No one has ever called me B, either. I like it," she said. "Hey, I saw you talking to Libby in the boat. Did she say anything about my idea?"

"Yeah, Allison is having doubts, but Libby likes it. They're going to talk more about it."

"I'm not surprised. She's worried about them being known only for their relationship. I tried to reassure her that we would spotlight their work and what they sacrificed."

"You can't do anything about it now, so let's not worry," said Krista. "Besides, I want to celebrate. I don't know if you've heard, but this incredible woman is in love with me and I love her back."

"Is that so," Brooke said, giggling.

"It is and tonight I'm showing her that love over and over," she said, her voice dropping low.

"Damn woman. You've made me weak just thinking about it."

Krista chuckled as they reached Brooke's cabin and pulled her inside. She pushed her up against the door and captured her lips. When they were both breathless she eased her lips from Brooke's. "That's what you have to look forward to tonight."

"Do we have to go?"

Krista smiled, her lips almost touching Brooke's. "Just for a bit." Then she kissed her again. This time their tongues danced and then battled as Krista pressed her body against Brooke, pinning her hands above her head against the door. She pulled back and looked into Brooke's eyes. They were so dark blue it reminded her of the night sky. She stared back at her with eyes just as dark.

Then she grabbed Brooke's hands and hurried them into the bedroom. Clothes flew around the room recklessly as they undressed with urgency.

Krista grabbed Brooke's hand and dragged her to the bed. She climbed up on her knees. "Face me, babe," she instructed. Brooke quickly followed.

Krista took her face in her hands and stared intensely into her eyes. "I love you, Brooke." Then she trailed her hands down over her breasts and cupped them, rubbing her thumbs over her nipples. She could see Brooke's chest rise and fall with her quickened breathing.

She then trailed her right hand down and cupped Brooke's sex while moving her other hand to her shoulder. She still stared into Brooke's eyes and then looked down and back up.

Brooke understood and mirrored Krista's movements. When she rubbed her thumbs over Krista's already hardened nipples she moaned. "Oh, how I love you, B."

It was Brooke's turn to trail her right hand down and over Krista's stomach, but she didn't stop. She moved her finger lower and ran it through Krista's wet center. Krista's eyes closed and she gasped.

Her eyes immediately reopened and locked onto Brooke's. "Together," she whispered as her finger ran through Brooke's wetness. "We're in this together," she said as she pushed two fingers inside Brooke. "Oh God, Brooke. I love being inside of you."

Brooke answered by easing two fingers inside Krista. When she felt Krista's velvety softness her eyes closed momentarily, savoring the incredible sensation. "I love you, Krissy," she groaned. "You are everything."

"Kiss me," Krista whispered.

Brooke pressed her lips to Krista's as she pushed her fingers in deeper. They made love with their mouths, tongues, hands, and fingers. They pulled one another close with their left hands and found a rhythm with their right hands.

Krista threw her head back. "Oh Brooke, I'm close." She pushed deeper into Brooke and curled her fingers. "Look at me, baby," she urged.

Brooke's eyes opened to see intense love staring back at her. She felt Krista tighten around her fingers and she did the same. "I love you, Krista," she cried. "I love you."

Krista's eyes softened as she fell over the edge. The orgasm seemed to pass through her into Brooke and back to her again. "Together," she mouthed.

They collapsed against one another and then fell over onto the bed both breathing heavily.

"So intense," Brooke said, still breathing hard.

"Just a couple of silly kids," Krista said lightly.

Brooke giggled and rolled over to face Krista. "In love."

"In love," Krista said, leaning over and kissing Brooke.

They lay in one another's arms lazing in the afterglow. Krista wasn't sure she'd ever been this happy. She loved creating Lovers Landing with Julia and her professional life was as busy as she wanted it, but falling in love with Brooke had made everything sweeter. She'd heard those clichés like 'you complete me' and had scoffed until now. What she felt, for the moment, was perfect. Everything was as it should be in her heart and in her life. She closed her eyes, snuggled closer and simply breathed.

"You're not going to sleep are you?" Brooke said softly.

"Nope. I'm living in this moment where there is nothing but you and me. No problems, no people, just us."

"Mmm, wish we never had to move then."

"We do, but not just now."

* * *

The nightly dancing and karaoke was in full swing. Everyone was there, some singing, some dancing, some drinking, and some eating. Krista looked around the bar and thought this was the best group they'd had so far. They all seemed to like one another, had fun together, and there had been no tension.

Allison and Libby didn't do everything with the group, but fit right in when they did. Anna, Shelley, Megan, and Renee appeared to have become friends and were even talking about vacationing together again.

The thing that surprised and made Krista the happiest was how they had all accepted Brooke. After that first day when Brooke dropped her guard and opened up they'd let her in. Each day as she showed more of her true self around not only Krista but also the group, they became even friendlier. And now you'd think this was a group of old friends having their usual good time.

She'd kept an eye on Tara because Lauren had danced with her several times and even when Tara wasn't trying she could be mesmerizing. Krista knew this all too well. It had taken several years, but she was glad they were friends and she knew she'd always be able to count on her.

"You have a very pleased look on your face," said Brooke.

Krista grinned at her. "I'm happy. Everyone is having a good time." She turned to Brooke. "Including me! How about you?"

"I'd be having a better time if you'd dance with me."

"I'd love to," Krista said, taking a quick drink and getting up.

"I've got to have the recipe to your Lesbian Licker," Brooke said and then laughed.

"Honey, you can have my Lesbian Licker anytime. But I'll also give you the recipe for the punch," Krista said, laughing with her.

They joined the others on the dance floor and when that song was over a slower one began. Krista had just put her arms around Brooke's shoulders when she felt a tap on hers. She turned around to find Allison and Libby.

"Brooke, would you mind if I danced with Krista?"

Brooke looked at Krista and said, "I don't if Krista doesn't mind."

Krista looked at Allison warily. "Okay." She let Brooke go and Allison offered her hand.

"I wanted to talk to you for a moment and thought this might be the best opportunity," Allison explained.

"What did you want to talk about?"

"The story, of course. I was thinking, this could've been you and Tara, you know."

"What?"

"If you and Tara would've stayed together, this story could've been about your relationship. You could be the dynamic couple that comes out to expose Hollywood's closeted bias and be the hero of the LGBTQ+ community."

"That wasn't my decision, Allison. Tara was ready and I wasn't. You and Libby are ready together. We didn't have that luxury."

"Are you sorry you waited?" asked Allison.

"No. I figure things worked out how they're supposed to. Besides, we're not as powerful as you and Libby, or as big of stars."

"You'd better not let Tara hear you say that."

Krista chuckled. "I'll say you're a liar if you tell her."

Allison laughed and then turned serious. "I'm not sure I want the responsibility Brooke's story may give us. The other way will make it a scandal that we've been found out and we can be the victims not saviors. I play the victim well."

"But Brooke isn't that journalist any longer. Do you have any idea how much that vitriol she receives hurts?"

"But she offers to do it."

"Not anymore," Krista said, shaking her head. "She wants to write stories like she described to you. What I know is that mine and Brooke's paths wouldn't have crossed and we wouldn't have had the opportunity to get to know one another, secrets included. And I would've missed out on the best thing that's ever happened to me. This change in Brooke gives us an opportunity for a life together."

"But what if I want her to do it the other way?"

"I don't think she'll do it. You know how talented she is."

"I do, that's why we want her."

"She wants to do different stories. Yours would be the first. Why would you want to be the victim, Allison? Why would you do that to her? " Krista was getting a bad feeling about Allison.

"You can't forget that Brooke is that person, Krista."

"Not anymore."

"I don't know. Deep down I think we are who we are and Brooke is the journalist she's been for the last ten years. She didn't just out someone once, Krista. Things happen to us along the way, I get that. But is the real Brooke the person you've fallen for in these few days or the one she's been all these years? Her history is against you, Krista."

"Why are you saying all this, Allison?" Krista asked defensively.

"Because you've always had this rosy outlook and shielded yourself from the bad parts of our business. It's there and you're right in the middle of it. We've all made sacrifices in one way or another. Brooke sacrificed her soul and got the reputation for it. You haven't and this dark side that she's put herself in is only going to hurt you."

"Dark side of our business or yourself? Is it your dark side hurting Brooke, too?"

"Not at all, I'm just warning you. The darkness is appealing to some as you know. Brooke's been there a long time."

"Well, she's chosen to get out."

"It's not as easy as you think, Krista," Allison said cryptically.

The song ended and Allison walked away.

"What the hell was that?" Krista mumbled to herself.

"You got a look at another side of Allison I see," Tara said, pulling Krista off the dance floor.

She looked around for Brooke and could see her laughing with Anna over at the table.

"Are you all right?" Tara asked.

Krista gathered herself and looked at Tara. "I'm not sure."

"She and Libby filled me in on Brooke's proposal. It's good, but I don't think Allison will go for it. I know about the part Megan offered you and what she said about Brooke, too. This is a peek at how things could be for you, Kris. What if Brooke changes her mind and writes it the other way? Have you thought about that?"

"No, because she says she doesn't want to write like that anymore."

"Allison can be very persuasive, Krista. You need to be prepared."

"I believe in her, Tara. You didn't see the pain she's been through and the change in her. She wants out. I trust her. And now I'm going stargazing with her. I've had enough of this for one night."

Tara raised her eyebrows questioningly.

"I'd invite you along, but…"

Tara chuckled. "Go have fun."

Krista went over and whispered in Brooke's ear. They quickly said their goodbyes and left.

27

"Wait here," Krista said, hurrying inside Brooke's cabin. She grabbed the blanket and pillows she'd left on a chair before they went to the bar.

"Let me help," Brooke said as Krista came back outside.

She let Brooke take the pillows. "Let's go down to your little beach. We can see better from there."

They laid the blanket out and plopped down on it with the pillows.

Krista released a big breath. "This is nice," she said, looking up at the twinkling stars.

"Are you going to tell me what's wrong?" asked Brooke, gazing at the night sky.

"Why would you ask that?"

"Because you haven't been the same since your dance with Allison. Did she upset you?"

Krista sighed and took Brooke's hand. "She just reminded me that our industry can be harsh. I was a bit surprised at her tone and didn't realize she had such a ruthless streak."

Brooke stroked the back of Krista's hand. "That's the side of Hollywood that I see the most."

"I know it's there, but that doesn't mean I have to be part of it."

"Me either—anymore."

Krista looked over at Brooke. "You mean that, right?"

Brooke's eyebrows climbed up her forehead. "Of course I mean that. You do believe me?"

"I do," Krista said, squeezing her hand. "I don't think Allison is going to agree with your idea for the story. I believe in you, Brooke. It'll be okay. We'll figure it out."

"You know, there's nothing we can do about any of this until Allison and Libby make a decision," Brooke said, bringing Krista's hand to her mouth and kissing the back of it. "It's a beautiful night, the stars are giving us a private light show and we're in love. Isn't that enough?"

Krista rolled on her side and cupped Brooke's face. "I don't think I'll ever get enough of you." She kissed Brooke tenderly and as the kiss deepened Krista forgot all about Allison Jennings.

* * *

Krista walked around the room. She couldn't believe she was so nervous for Brooke. Actually, it felt good. It meant she cared. She remembered feeling more nervous for Tara when she was waiting for a part than when she was for herself. She loved Brooke and wanted her to be happy; it was that simple.

They had both been a tad subdued that day while waiting on Allison and Libby to make their decision. The vacation was almost over. This was their last day and night. In the morning it was back to the airport and then to LA. She and Brooke hadn't really talked about what was next, but planned to later that night.

She was beginning to get a good feeling since Brooke had been gone so long. Surely if they didn't want Brooke to write the piece it wouldn't take long to say no. But there was something about Allison that worried Krista; she had heard that she could be a diva. Any woman that was successful and confident in their field would one time or another be labeled a diva or something similar. However, she couldn't shake the sinister undertones of their conversation from last night.

Krista sighed and decided to sit outside to wait on Brooke. She had been pacing the cabin and outside she could at least walk down to the water and get her feet wet. The water always calmed her and gave her a sense of peace.

When she walked out the back door she saw Brooke sitting in one of the chairs next to the fire pit. "Hey babe, when did you get back?" she asked cheerfully, walking toward her. When she saw Brooke's face she knew something was wrong. "Oh no. What happened?"

"They didn't go for it," she said softly, looking up at Krista.

Brooke looked so hurt and the pain in her eyes tore at Krista's heart. She kneeled and said, "It's okay, you'll write about someone else. You have lots of ideas about other people that caught your attention, right? People that you can tell an honest and inspiring story about."

Brooke stared at her and then said, "Let's go inside."

She got up and took Krista's hand and they walked into the cabin. Once inside she dropped her hand and walked over to the couch. "They want me to do the article like I did the others," she said, not looking at Krista.

"But you don't want to write like that anymore," Krista said, beginning to get an uneasy feeling.

Brooke looked up at her. "I said I'd do it."

"What?" Krista said quietly, unbelieving. "Why?"

"It will be the last one. After that no more deception and sleaze," Brooke said, trying to convince Krista as well as herself.

"No, Brooke. You said yourself that an article like that, about such loved stars, would cause a shit storm bigger than any of the others. You'd never be seen as anything but that kind of journalist. Please don't do this."

Brooke looked away and said softly, "It will be okay."

"How can you say that? Do you have any idea how much venom will be spewed about you? Allison and Libby will be the little darlings. Please don't do this," Krista pleaded, trying to talk Brooke out of it.

When Brooke didn't say anything Krista asked softly, "Did you think of me? I don't expect you to make professional decisions based on our relationship, but…"

"Of course I thought of you," Brooke said, meeting her eyes.

Krista sat down next to her. "Then how am I supposed to sit and watch people tear you apart and say hateful things about you when I know they are based on untruths? How am I supposed to see the hurt in your eyes and not be able to do anything about it?" Krista said, her voice catching.

"I'll be all right."

Krista cradled Brooke's face between her hands. "Please don't do this, B," she begged.

Tears pooled in Brooke's eyes.

Krista kissed her cheek. "Please don't do it." She kissed her other cheek as tears stung her own eyes and repeated, "Please, B." Then she softly kissed her lips and pleaded one more time. "Please, baby. Don't."

Brooke didn't say anything and Krista dropped her hands and slowly got up.

She swiped at the fallen tears on her cheeks and faced Brooke. "I can't watch you do this, Brooke. I can't watch you punish yourself again. I thought you loved me."

"I do," Brooke said, tears falling down her cheeks now.

"Then how am I supposed to watch you hurt yourself? I would be a part of it and I can't do that. I will not be part of you hurting yourself when it doesn't have to be that way. I won't do it," Krista said, raising her voice and walking toward the door.

"Where are you going?" Brooke said, standing up.

Krista shook her head and walked out the door without saying another word.

* * *

Krista walked in the back door of the kitchen and slipped through to the office. The last thing she wanted was to run into Allison, Libby, or anyone else. She absolutely couldn't stay in that cabin with Brooke one more minute and had walked out with only her phone in her pocket. She'd used the hidden key to get in the office and found what she was looking for.

She grabbed a six pack of beer out of the kitchen refrigerator and could hear the music playing in the bar. No doubt everyone was having one more party before leaving in the morning. Sneaking out the back door, she walked to the far edge of their property and unlocked the door to a cabin they hadn't finished yet. It was liveable, but not for guests.

After putting the beer in the refrigerator she took two bottles with her, grabbed a chair off the porch and went down to sit by the water. Her tears had stopped falling by the time she'd gotten to the office, but they were back again.

Why would Brooke do this? Off and on all day they had talked about what she would do if Allison and Libby said no. Krista had supported her, encouraged her, and loved her all day. Did Brooke still think she didn't deserve happiness?

She downed half of one of the bottles of beer and called Julia. As soon as she heard Julia's voice the tears came again along with a lump in her throat.

"Hey sweetness," Julia said, answering the phone. She'd overheard Brooke call her this and it was now her favorite way to tease Krista.

Krista tried to gather herself to speak.

"Krissy, what's wrong?" Julia said, immediately concerned.

"Oh Jules," Krista said, sniffling.

"What happened?"

"Allison and Libby didn't agree to Brooke's idea for the article. They want her to write it portraying them as victims."

"No one says she has to do it!" said Julia, defending Brooke.

"I know, but she agreed to do it anyway."

"Why?"

"I don't know. She said it would be the last one, but she'll never be able to come back from it."

"Where are you, Krista?"

"I couldn't be part of it, Jules. I can't watch her punish herself this way. I thought she could see her value now. I would do anything for her, but I can't sit by and do nothing, Jules," Krista sobbed.

"Krista!" Julia said firmly. "Where are you?"

"I'm at number 5," she said between breaths.

"Number 5? It's not finished."

"It's fine. I didn't want to be near anyone."

"Okay. Give me thirty minutes and I'll be there," said Julia.

"No! I need you to take the group to the airport in the morning. I'm going to stay here and cry all night. By the time you get back I'll be at the beach waiting."

"Let me come now."

"No. I've got to think all this through. We'll talk when you get back tomorrow."

"What about Brooke?"

"What about Brooke? I obviously can't reach her," Krista said as a fresh round of tears began to fall. "And that breaks my heart," she cried.

"Oh Krissy. I can't stand this. Let me come to you."

"Please Jules. I really need to sit here alone."

"Okay. I'll check on you in the morning."

"Thanks. I love you."

"I love you, too."

Krista ended the call and opened the other beer. After she'd drank half of it her tears dried up and she got angry. Why couldn't Allison and Libby be brave? What were they afraid of? And why would Brooke do this when she didn't have to?

She gazed out over the water into the darkness and drank the rest of her beer. Her thoughts were dark and then hopeful and then dark again. At one point she went in and got two more beers. This time she sat in the rocking chair on the back porch and drank and cried and tried to figure out why Brooke couldn't trust their love.

She began to look back over the last couple of weeks. When Presley told her Brooke had made a reservation she didn't panic. They went to work and Presley supplied her with enough information to get an idea of who Brooke was. The memory of meeting her in the diner brought fresh tears to her eyes as well as a warmness to her heart.

The last week replayed in her head as Brooke opened up to her and then she touched her lips remembering that first kiss. Damnit, she was in love with Brooke! It couldn't end as quickly as it started.

"I've got to figure this out," she said aloud. "I can't lose her."

28

The next morning Brooke was banging on the door to Krista's cabin when Tara finally opened it.

"What the fuck, Brooke."

"I need to see Krista," she demanded.

"She's not here," Tara said.

"Don't lie to me, Tara. I've got to talk to her."

"Brooke, I haven't seen her since we were at the beach yesterday morning. What's the matter?"

Brooke fidgeted from one foot to the other and looked around her and finally sighed. "I messed up, Tara. Bad!"

"Is it Allison?"

Brooke nodded.

"Look Brooke, I don't know what Allison asked you to do. And I don't know what you think you're giving up for Krista, but it doesn't matter. Krista's worth it."

"I know that! That's why I need to find her. I'm going to Allison and Libby's to tell them I won't write the article. I don't care if I never write another word, as long as we're together." Tears filled Brooke's eyes. "I know being with me will be hard, but I believe in us and

Krista kept telling me we can get through anything as long as we're together."

"I've never seen her as happy as she is with you. I'll find her. You go to Allison. Meet me at the bar when you're finished. Julia will know where she is."

Brooke stood there nodding and quickly wiped away a tear.

"What are you waiting on? Go!" Tara said.

Brooke took off with Tara close behind her.

When Tara got to the restaurant she went through to the office. "Hey," she said, walking in to find Julia behind the desk. "Have you seen Krista?"

Julia studied her before answering. "I haven't seen her this morning."

"You know what happened then. We need to find her. Brooke is at Allison's calling off whatever deal she made with the devil."

"She is!" Julia said, standing up.

"Do you know where Krista is?"

Julia shook her head and hurried out of the office with Tara right behind her. She stopped in the restaurant where Becca and Courtney were scrolling on their phones.

"Courtney, I need you to check the bikes and make sure they're all there. Text me when you've counted them," Julia told her.

Courtney looked at her hesitantly, but marched out the door.

"Becca, run down to the dock and get one of the paddle boards out, please. Wait there until you hear from me."

"Okay, Mom," she said. "Is everything all right?"

"It will be. Hurry, honey."

Becca rushed out the door without looking back.

"Do you know where she is?" asked Tara.

"No, but I have an idea."

A few minutes passed and Julia's phone pinged. She looked down at it.

"Well?" Tara asked anxiously.

"All the bikes are there."

"What now?"

Before Julia could answer her phone pinged again. She read it and looked at Tara. "One of the paddle boards is gone, so that tells me Krissy is on the water."

Brooke came in the door and walked toward them with purpose in her stride. "Julia, do you know where Krista is?"

Julia stared at Brooke for a few moments with her hands on her hips.

"Please Julia. I've made a mess. I'm sure she told you that. I'm trying to make it right," Brooke said desperately.

"She did tell me, Brooke. How are you planning to make it right? Because I'm not going to let you hurt her all over again."

"I'm trusting her. She told me to trust in our love, but I was afraid I'd drag her down. I know now that I was wrong. Please tell me where she is."

"I don't know for sure, but I think she's at her little beach where you rode bikes to a few days ago."

"Can I use a paddle board?"

"Do you know how to get there?"

Brooke nodded. "She showed me two days ago. It's quicker than a bike."

Julia nodded. "Becca has a paddle board waiting for you."

Brooke started to leave when Julia stopped her.

"Brooke, it's okay to be afraid. She is too. But she's willing to fight for you. She has from the moment you made that reservation. Will you fight for her?"

"Yes! That's what I'm doing. I'm fighting for us."

"Make her see that. Make her see you're in this together."

"I will. Thanks Julia. Thanks Tara," she said over her shoulder as she ran out of the restaurant.

"She'd better get this right," Tara said.

Julia sighed. "Krista believes in her, so I guess we should too."

* * *

Krista leaned back on her hands and looked out over the little inlet. She could see the main lake, but the peace she usually got from the water wasn't working this morning. She'd been up before the sun, walking and thinking.

When she couldn't quiet her anxious mind she went to the dock and took off on her paddle board. Without thinking she'd paddled to the little beach she knew so well. This used to be her place to solve any problems, rest from busy days, or just enjoy being near the water.

But now it felt different. Memories of Brooke were everywhere. That incredible first kiss took place in the water just beyond where her feet rested in the sand. She could hear their laughter and could almost feel Brooke's hand in hers. Krista sighed.

She didn't have much time until Brooke would be leaving for the airport. All she knew was that she couldn't let her get on that plane. She hadn't figured out how to convince her to stay though.

Her tears had finally dried up, but her heart ached in her chest. She closed her eyes and lifted her face to the sun as thoughts kept swirling through her head. The familiar sound of a paddle rhythmically slicing through the water barely reached her ears, even as it began to get louder.

She opened her eyes and squinted through the sun to see a lone paddler coming her way. Her heart leapt in her chest sensing it was Brooke. She continued to watch her paddle, but didn't move.

Brooke dropped to her knees as the board glided into the sand. She quickly got off and walked to her.

Krista was reminded of the day in the diner when Brooke came toward her and her heart had raced. Brooke stopped in front of her, blocking the sun from her eyes. She looked down at her with a mixture of regret and hope on her face.

"Please forgive me," she said, falling down on her knees in front of Krista. "No one has ever fought for me. You have tried to make me see that I'm worth it. When I stopped and realized that you know the struggles we're going to face, but you still want to be with me, I understood what you meant when you told me we could do anything together. Please Krista, don't give up on me."

Tears pooled in Krista's eyes. Before she could say anything Brooke reached for her hand. "I probably won't ever believe I'm worth it, but I know you are and I know we are. There is no way in this world that I'm writing that article. It makes me sick to think I even considered it."

"Did Allison threaten you?" Krista asked quietly.

"Not exactly," Brooke said, shaking her head and looking down at their hands. "I'm such an idiot."

"No you're not!" Krista said, grabbing Brooke's chin and raising it so she could see her eyes.

Brooke smiled. "See! You're always fighting for me. Allison made it seem like there was no way we could be together; that your career would be ruined and we wouldn't be accepted. She made me think that I would be protecting you by leaving you. Because deep down, I knew you couldn't stay with me if I wrote that article. So I said yes because I didn't want you to be hurt. And what did I do? I hurt you more than any tabloid or Hollywood gossip monger could. It was just so confusing and seemed hopeless. But last night your voice kept going through my head that we could do anything together. I believe you," Brooke said, sighing. "I believe you," she said again as tears spilled from her eyes.

Krista sat up on her knees and pulled Brooke to her, holding her close. Her heart was still racing, but now with relief that she had Brooke in her arms where she belonged. And she could feel Brooke's strong arms wrapped around her, no longer doubtful or unsure, but solid and lasting.

After several moments Krista pulled back and looked into Brooke's eyes. "I shouldn't have walked away from you last night. I'm sorry. I will never do that again."

"That's what it took to make me see we could do anything as long as we were together."

"I should've realized Allison did something to you, B. I was so shocked I couldn't think and it took a while for me to see there was more to it. I wasn't going to let you get on that plane today," she said with a smile. "I didn't know what I was going to say, but I wasn't giving up."

"I know things will be hard for us because of my reputation, but I'll do whatever it takes. I don't want you to suffer because of me."

"I'm not going to suffer because of you! I love you, Brooke! Not being with you is inconceivable. Let's stop worrying about things that haven't happened."

Brooke smiled then and said, "Okay. Then, can I have a job?"

Krista's brow furrowed. "What?"

"I'm pretty sure since I told Allison and Libby that I wouldn't be writing their article, my journalist days are numbered. So I'm going to need a job."

Krista threw her head back and laughed. "Honey, Allison Jennings ain't the only one with power in Hollywood, but I do have a job for you."

"What's that?" Brooke chuckled.

"Kiss me," she said as the smile fell from her face.

Brooke crashed her lips to Krista's, nearly knocking them over. She softened the kiss but her arms were still tightly wrapped around Krista. "Sorry," she breathed. "I was afraid I'd never get to do that again."

"Oh B," Krista said, stroking the side of Brooke's face and looking at her tenderly. "I told you, right here on this beach, I don't ever want you to stop kissing me."

Brooke stared into Krista's blue eyes that sparkled once again. "I love you, Krissy. I love you so much." Then she leaned in and claimed Krista's lips once more; this time with love, passion, and promise.

Krista deepened the kiss and their tongues did the dance that filled their hearts with love. After several moments Krista pulled away and looked into Brooke's eyes. She could see the once tortured woman was gone and the woman Krista loved the most shone through.

"Promise me you'll never doubt our love again," she said softly.

"I never doubted our love; I just didn't know how strong it was."

Krista kissed her softly and grinned. "The make up sex we're going to have will be beyond incredible, but right now we've got to get back."

"What?" Brooke said, startled out of her blissful kissing haze.

"We've got to catch the group before they leave."

"We do?"

"Yeah babe, there's something I've got to do before they go." Krista kissed her again.

"Okay," Brooke said.

"Come on. Race you," Krista said, running to her paddle board. Before pushing it into the water she turned around and hugged Brooke fiercely. "Thank you for finding me."

"Oh sweetness, thank you for not giving up."

With a kiss Brooke let her go and they both got on their boards and began paddling. Once they were back in the main part of the lake Krista paddled up next to Brooke. "Are you sure you don't need to fly back today?"

"We didn't get a chance to talk about what comes next last night. But no, I don't have to go back today."

"Okay, just making sure. We can have that talk later."

Lovers Landing's dock came into sight. They could see the van parked next to the restaurant where Becca and Courtney were loading the group's bags.

"Do you have to go to the airport with them?" Brooke asked.

"Not this time," Krista said, sliding to a stop. She walked up onto the sand and turned around to reach for Brooke's hand.

Brooke squeezed Krista's hand. "I love holding your hand."

Krista gave her a sideways glance and smirked. "I know."

Julia and Tara walked toward them before they reached the van.

"You're holding hands. That's a good sign," Julia said.

"Thanks Julia. You were right. She was on the beach. And thank you Tara for everything," Brooke said.

Krista looked over at her. "You'll have to tell me about that later."

"Nothing to tell, Kris. She was frantic to find you and I helped." Tara shrugged.

Krista smiled at her and then looked past them as Allison and Libby were about to get on the van.

"Allison," she called, dropping Brooke's hand and walking over to them.

Allison turned around and waited as Krista walked up. When Krista was face to face with her she reached up and slapped her hard. Allison's head whipped around and she stumbled, but Libby caught her while the others looked on and gasped and murmured, "Oh my God!"

"You should be ashamed of yourself. Just because you're afraid doesn't mean you have to ruin someone else's life or relationship. You don't deserve the piece Brooke was going to do on you and Libby."

"You're exactly right," Allison said, rubbing her cheek.

The group gasped again. "What?"

"I now realize that we have to stand up for one another," she said, looking over at Libby affectionately. "We shouldn't have to hide or come out when it's best for our careers. And it will stay that way if we don't speak up. Libby so graciously pointed out to me it's time for us to stop being fearful. I know you created this place so people could come here and safely be who they are. Hopefully someday, we can put you out of business and places like this won't be needed."

Libby put her arm around Allison's shoulders and encouraged her. "Go on, Ali."

Allison looked at Brooke. "I'm sorry for the way I talked to you yesterday and again this morning, Brooke. I do know your talent and Krista seems to think we could really help our community with this grand coming out piece you envisioned. If you would still be willing to create it, we'd love to do it."

Krista and Brooke looked at one another.

"Oh, and whether you do or not, Libby and I will use whatever influence we have to shut down the gossip about your relationship with Krista."

"What about the movie?" Brooke asked, looking at Allison and then over at Megan.

"The movie?" Krista said, looking at Allison. She then realized

Allison must have told Brooke about Megan's offer. "Oh honey," she said to Brooke. "No offense Megan, but how do I know this isn't going to be another low rate movie where maybe this time they don't kill off the lesbian lead?"

"You weren't losing a part because of me?" Brooke asked Krista.

"No!" she said. She narrowed her eyes at Allison and really wanted to slap her again.

"What do we do now?" Libby said, trying to ease the tension.

Brooke rested her arm on Krista's shoulder and looked around at the group. "I'll email you a proposed concept tonight," she said to Libby.

"All right," Libby agreed.

A smile began to grow on Krista's face. "I've got an idea."

29

"Everyone, come with me," Krista said, leading them into the bar. "Have a seat."

When they were all seated she began. "It seems to me if we want to make a movie that is entertaining and represents who we are then we need to make it ourselves."

"What?" said Allison.

"I agree with you, Krissy," said Tara.

"We have very good producers right here," she said, nodding to Anna and Shelley. "Plus a talented director," she said, pointing at Megan. "Look at the acting talent in this room. Renee, Allison, Libby, Tara, and me! That would be an all star cast," she said, grinning and spreading her arms out.

The others were smiling and looking at one another while Krista continued. "But we can't do a thing if we don't have an awesome story and a brilliant writer to create it."

She looked lovingly at Brooke. "Would you write it, B?"

Brooke smiled at Krista, her eyes wide and looked around at the others. "I'd do anything for you," she said to Krista.

"Everyone get out your phones and pull up your schedules," Krista instructed them.

"Let's meet back here one month from today. That will be the first meeting of the Lovers Landing Production Company. Bring your ideas for the story. We are going to make the first blockbuster LGBTQ+ movie. Are you in?"

"Hell yeah," said Anna and Shelley together.

"We're in," said Libby, grinning at Allison.

"I get to direct?" asked Megan.

Krista looked at Renee and shook her head. "It's always the director that tries to run things," she teased. "Yes, Megan."

"Then I'm in."

Tara looked up with hesitation. "Are you sure about this, Krissy? I mean I just got here."

"Of course I'm sure, Tara. Any objections?" Krista said to the group.

No one complained.

"Count me in," Tara said with a grin.

"I think that's everyone." Krista turned to Julia. "You know we're going to need you to run the business end of things."

Julia nodded. "It's not like I have anything else to do." They all laughed and clapped.

"Okay then. Y'all had better load up or you're going to miss your plane," said Krista.

They dispersed and boarded the van, all talking excitedly about the new production company.

Julia smiled at Krista as the last person got on the van. "Since everything is okay now, are you sure you don't want to go with me to the airport?"

"I'm sure," said Krista, grabbing Brooke's hand and walking toward her cabin.

Julia and Tara watched them walk away. Tara said, "That is the most unlikely match."

"I think they've been waiting on one another for a long time. Brooke has a chance at a new life and Krista is finally living hers," said Julia.

Krista stopped walking when they reached the back porch and

faced Brooke. "I want you to hold my hand at our movie premiere," Krista said.

Brooke's eyebrows raised up her forehead. "Our movie premiere?"

"Yes, it's going to happen."

"Okay."

"I want you to hold my hand when we get married."

"Married?" Brooke said, swallowing.

"I'll surprise you one of these days with a proposal, but it's going to happen."

"Can't wait," Brooke said softly.

"I want you to hold my hand when I'm old," Krista said earnestly.

Brooke's face softened. "I'll be right beside you."

"We couldn't write a better Hollywood ending." Krista winked, kissed Brooke gently, and then pulled her inside.

THREE YEARS LATER

"We are here on the red carpet talking to the stars as they make their way inside for this year's Academy Awards. Krista, over here." Ryan Seacrest, the red carpet host, waved at Krista and Brooke.

"Hey Ryan," Krista said, beaming, walking over hand in hand with Brooke. "Isn't this exciting!"

"It is. I'm so glad to see you."

"It's good to see you. I'm not sure you've met my partner. This is Brooke Bell," Krista said, absolutely glowing at Brooke.

"Hello Brooke, so very nice to meet you," Ryan said. "Tell me Brooke, how does it feel to be nominated for best screenplay?"

Brooke grinned. "It's incredible and unbelievable."

"Krista, you have to be proud of the movie and all the nominations it's received. How did it come about? Was this an idea you had for a long time?"

"Not exactly, Ryan. I was with a group of friends and we dreamed of a time when same sex relationships would be the norm. What better way to make that happen than to see it on the big screen. The majority of movies and TV shows portraying the LGBTQ+ community missed the mark. So we set out to make a movie that was authentic, realistic, and *good*," she said, emphasizing the last word.

"You did that and more. What's next for this group of friends that I know is now your production company?"

"We have several projects in the works and you'll see something on TV from us very soon."

"Hey look! Is this more of your gang coming up?" Ryan asked.

Krista and Brooke turned to see Allison and Libby walking toward them.

"Where's the big party after the show tonight?" Ryan asked them. They all looked at one another. "Or is it a secret?"

Allison answered with a cagey look. "We know a place where all our secrets are safe."

* * *

The next evening on one of the tables in the bar at Lovers Landing sat a variety of Oscars, Golden Globes, and SAG awards.

"Isn't this awesome!" Krista exclaimed to the group. Everyone applauded. "Last night we added to the awards for our movie with Best Picture! And Best Director for Megan." Everyone applauded again. "And Best Screenplay for my beautiful girl, Brooke."

After the applause quieted Krista looked at the group before her and said, "There's one more thing. We wanted to invite y'all to our wedding."

"What? Now?" a few people asked.

Krista grinned and squeezed Brooke's hand. "It's so hard to get everyone together and we already had the party planned so we decided this was a good time to get married."

"Down on the beach, let's go," Julia said.

Everyone jumped up and followed Julia and Heidi down to the beach where chairs were waiting and flowers adorned a small arch. There were speakers set up and "Got No Choice" by Brooke Eden was playing in the background.

Krista and Brooke waited hand in hand on the deck behind the restaurant while the others settled in the chairs on the beach.

"It was almost four years ago that Julia and I sat right here talking about our dreams to make this a place where people could be themselves. And look at you, my love," she said, cupping Brooke's face. "You're marrying me and we're living our best life. An ending even Hollywood would love."

"We're ready," Julia called to them.

Krista took Brooke's hand in hers and they walked toward happily ever after.

ABOUT THE AUTHOR

Small town Texas girl that grew up believing she could do anything. Her mother loved to read and romance novels were a favorite that she passed on to her daughter. She found lesfic novels and her world changed. She not only fell in love with the genre, but wanted to write her own stories. You can find her books on Amazon and her website at jameymoodyauthor.com.

You can email her at jameymoodyauthor@gmail.com

As an independent publisher a review is greatly appreciated and I would be grateful if you could take the time to write just a few words.

Below is a list of my other books with links that will take you to their page. And after that I've included the first chapter of *One Little Yes* for your enjoyment.

ALSO BY JAMEY MOODY

Live This Love

The Your Way Series:
Finding Home
Finding Family
Finding Forever

It Takes A Miracle
One Little Yes

ONE LITTLE YES

Chapter 1

"What are you waiting on?" Gina Gray questioned the universe loudly while spreading her arms out wide and looking upward. She sighed, put her phone on the table and walked to the window of her apartment.

Looking out on her little piece of New York City, she watched people hurrying down the street, living their lives. Christmas decorations dotted the street lights and entrances to the other buildings. There were lights that would twinkle behind various windows across the street as the sun went down.

If she opened the window she'd hear the sounds of life from below. The cold air would pillow around her face and if she was lucky the aroma of fresh bread from the bakery down the street might waft through her apartment.

She usually loved Christmas, but not so much this year. Her father was back in Texas in an assisted living center and she wasn't able to go home. These were the times when she missed her mother the most. She'd been gone five years now and sometimes it felt like yesterday, others it felt like decades. Her parents had tried to have kids for years and thought it wasn't going to happen and then surprise, there she was. Even though they were older she'd had a good childhood and they were at every sporting event, play, choir concert, and anything else she participated in.

A familiar sound came from her phone announcing a text message. She walked over and picked it up and read the message. Then she walked to the buzzer next to the front door and pushed the button that unlocked the door below to allow entrance to the building. A few minutes later there was a knock at the door.

Gina opened it to let her best friend, Shannon, in. "Why are you here?" asked Gina.

Shannon walked in and pulled a bottle of wine out of the sack she was carrying and set it on the cabinet in the kitchen. She took two glasses down and rifled around in a drawer for the wine opener. "You had a doctor's appointment today. Of course I'm going to be here." She opened the bottle and poured each of them a glass. After handing one to Gina, she walked over to the couch and sat down. "So? What did they say?" she asked, taking a sip from her glass.

Gina joined her on the couch and took a sip of the wine. "Mmm, this is good!" she exclaimed, looking at her glass.

"You don't drink very often so when you do it should be good," Shannon said matter-of-factly. She waited patiently.

"Just as I've always known would eventually happen, having been diagnosed with kidney disease at sixteen, I need a kidney transplant."

"And?"

"And it needs to be sooner rather than later."

"Okay. Let's find you a donor, then," Shannon said.

"I hope it's as easy as you make it sound. You do realize I don't have any siblings."

"I seem to remember growing up together that it was just you and me. Duh!" she teased, rolling her eyes.

"My good kidney, and I use that term loosely, is failing. Dialysis is in my future if I can't find a donor," she said, dropping her head to her chest. She sighed and looked back up with tears in her eyes. "I really hoped I'd never have to do that."

Shannon set her glass down and scooted closer to Gina, putting her arm around her shoulders and grabbing her free hand with her own. "Then we'll find you a donor before that happens."

Gina loved Shannon like she could only imagine a sister would. She sank into her comfort for a few moments before sitting up and taking another sip of her wine. "You know it's one thing to find a match, but it's a whole other thing to find someone willing to give up their kidney."

"I'd do it in a heartbeat," Shannon said quickly.

"I know you would, but you love me."

"I sure do and I'll tell you right now if Travis is a match, I'll make him give you one of his," Shannon said, sipping her wine. Travis was Shannon's boyfriend and when they'd started dating, he and Gina had become fast friends. "Actually, I wouldn't have to make him; you know he loves you too."

Gina chuckled. "Lucky for you, I love women or I think Travis might be my boyfriend."

Shannon laughed. "There's my girl! Look GG, it's okay to be upset today. You didn't get the best news from the doctor. Let's enjoy this wine and order some food. Besides, we have Christmas in a few days and I promise you it'll be merry even though we can't go home this year."

"I know, Shan. Thanks. I can always count on you."

"And after that, Travis's and my New Year's party will be the best! We will find you a donor there. I promise," Shannon stated.

"Careful with those promises," Gina warned.

"You let me worry about that. We're having our friends, but also people from my work and from Travis's. It's a done deal."

Gina loved Shannon's optimism, but she knew it was going to be a lot harder than that.

"Come on, Gina," Shannon said, snapping her out of her thoughts. "I'm in media. I'll design a campaign if I have to."

Gina chuckled. "I hadn't thought of that. I can see billboards in

Times Square now." Gina put her arm up waving from left to right, looking at an imaginary billboard. "'Be kind, give this girl a kidney.'"

Shannon frowned. "Ugh no! That's why I'm the creative one."

"Well, this problem solver," Gina said, pointing to herself. "Has a ton of work to do before Christmas. This just happens to be the busiest time of the year. We've got to get those packages delivered."

"You know," Shannon said, an idea forming in her head. "You manage a very large team with a lot of people under them."

"I don't like that look on your face. I can tell what you're thinking. Give the boss a kidney, get a promotion."

Shannon laughed. "Not exactly. You have a huge network of people in your distribution chain. There's no reason not to use that resource if you have to. You may have to think out of the box, so to speak, even though your business is delivering boxes." Shannon laughed at her own play on words.

Gina chuckled and shook her head.

"Let's move on to more important things," Shannon said.

"What's more important than saving my life with a kidney?"

"Saving your love life. You haven't been on a date in forever."

"Are you kidding me! You know how busy I am this time of year. And let me tell you one more time that people don't like to date sick people."

"GG, you are an extremely beautiful, smart, and talented person. You don't have to tell someone your medical history to fool around and have a little fun."

"And here I thought you were continually setting me up so that I could find a partner. Which is it?"

"I want you to find the happiness I have with Travis. Is that such a bad thing?"

Gina sighed. "No, it's just hard, Shan. How can I not tell someone that I have a medical condition that could kill me or at least limit my quality of life."

"But you don't even give them a chance," Shannon said, pleading. "What about the woman I set you up with a few months ago from our legal department?"

"Her name is Kim and she was very busy, just like me. When she happened to see all the pill bottles in my cabinet, I had to explain so she wouldn't think I was some kind of drug supplier."

"Wait, what was she doing in your cabinet?"

"I told you all about it, remember?" Gina looked at her pointedly.

"You did not! Did she spend the night?" Shannon said, her voice rising.

"I told you she did and then when I explained the situation she listened and we went out one other time and that was that."

"But she seemed like a stand up person. Why didn't you tell me this, GG?"

Gina sighed. "I really thought I did. We talked about what I was expecting with my health and she was very honest. She really is busy and her career is very important to her; she wasn't in a place to start a relationship, much less take care of someone else."

"So she was open to meeting up and having sex, just not more than that?"

"Nope. She liked me and felt like it would become more. But my *more* has some added problems that come with it."

"I swear you didn't tell me this," Shannon said, her brow furrowed. "That must be why she asked about you a couple of weeks ago," she said to herself. She turned to Gina. "I ran into her and she asked how you were doing. I didn't think anything about it because I thought you didn't hit it off. Hmm, I guess you made an impression."

"Well, it's not often you spend the night with someone and find out the next morning they need a kidney."

"Do you want to tell me the real reason why you didn't say anything about this?" Shannon said, pressing Gina.

She hesitated for a moment. "It made me sad. It showed me that there's no way anyone is going to want to be with me when I have this going on. I knew you'd try to cheer me up and tell me I'm wrong, but this time I'm not, Shan. This is my life. Just me, no partner, no girlfriend—hell, not even a date."

Shannon put her glass down and grabbed Gina by her shoulders and looked her in the eye. "It's not always going to be that way. And please, don't do that again. Of course I'm going to try to make it better, but if you don't want to hear it then tell me. Just please don't think you're going through this alone, because you have me. We've always had each other. Always."

Gina smiled. "Okay, I won't do it again. And I know you're always with me. It's just that it feels like you're the one that's had to do all the heavy lifting."

"Oh darling. We don't keep score. Please remember back to middle school and then to high school. Who took care of me? You did! It's just the way it works sometimes. Okay?"

"Okay," Gina said, pulling Shannon into a hug. "I'm so glad I've got you."

"Me too."

Gina's phone beeped, pulling them apart. She read the text and groaned. "A delivery disaster just in time for Christmas." She turned to Shannon. "Will you order us food? I have to take care of this. Hopefully it won't take long."

"Go solve Santa's sleigh problems. I'll order." Shannon got up and opened the drawer with the take-out menus while Gina went to her desk and opened her laptop.

Get One Little Yes

Printed in Great Britain
by Amazon